Front Office Nurse

Ruth Dorset

THORNDIKE
CHIVERS

This Large Print edition is published by Thorndike Press®, Waterville, Maine USA and by BBC Audiobooks, Ltd, Bath, England.

Published in 2004 in the U.S. by arrangement with Maureen Moran Agency.

Published in 2005 in the U.K. by arrangement with the author.

U.S. Hardcover 0-7862-7160-4 (Candlelight)
U.K. Hardcover 1-4056-3216-X (Chivers Large Print)
U.K. Softcover 1-4056-3217-8 (Camden Large Print)

The text of this Large Print edition is unabridged.
Other aspects of the book may vary from the original edition.

Set in 16 pt. Plantin by Christina S. Huff.

Printed in the United States on permanent paper.

British Library Cataloguing-in-Publication Data available

Library of Congress Cataloging-in-Publication Data

Dorset, Ruth, 1912–
    Front office nurse / by Ruth Dorset.
        p. cm.
    ISBN 0-7862-7160-4 (lg. print : hc : alk. paper)
    1. Nurses — Fiction. 2. Physicians — Fiction. 3. Large type books. I. Title.
PR9199.3.R5996F76 2004
    813'.54—dc22   2004046233

To a long time friend and Mentor
— C. R. Mersereau

Chapter One

The heavy, determined sound of footsteps coming into the office alerted Nurse Rita Lewis to approaching trouble even before she looked up to see who it was. It had been a long, difficult day at her front office desk, and the best of an early summer afternoon was not helping. With a sigh she glanced up to see who it was. And her spirits did not rise when she found herself staring into the face of Morton Gordon, Jr., the most overweight and ill-tempered of all the hospital board.

She forced a smile. "Yes, Mr. Gordon?"

"I've come to ask why my sister hasn't been admitted," Morton Gordon, Jr. said wrathfully. "I understand she's been put off for more than a week!" The middle-aged son of a wealthy father, Morton Gordon, Jr. was president of the city's largest industry, the Gordon Pulp Mills.

Rita said: "Let me check my list," and she opened a loose-leaf filing book.

Morton Gordon, Jr.'s bulldog face was

purple and oozing perspiration. "I fail to see why that is necessary. She phoned only thirty minutes ago."

Rita was well aware of this, as she'd taken the call herself, but she had wanted to put on a suitable show for the board member. She looked up at him again, still with a polite smile. "We offered Mrs. Barry ward accommodation, but she refused it."

Morton Gordon, Jr. exploded. "Ward accommodation! I should think she would refuse it. Is this the gratitude the hospital shows my family after all the years of service we've given it, not to mention the financial support we've given and are giving!"

"It has nothing to do with service or financial support, Mr. Gordon," Rita said quietly. "It's a matter of rooms. We just haven't got the space."

He scowled at her. "I don't believe it."

"It's true."

He pointed an accusing finger at her. "Don't tell me you haven't some empty rooms. I happen to know!"

Rita nodded agreement, her pretty face taking on an expression of cool disinterest. She was blonde and had an unusually even disposition that made her suited to this difficult desk job. She said: "It's true we do have several private rooms empty. But this is our general practice. We have to reserve them for emergencies."

"My sister is ill," he retorted. "Isn't that an emergency?"

"According to the listing I have here, Dr. Solomon wants to hospitalize her for observation of a migraine headache problem," Rita said. "That hardly rates as something urgent."

Morton Gordon, Jr. shook his balding head in frustration. "Mrs. Barry is planning a trip overseas later in the summer. She wants to get this over with."

Rita shrugged. "I'm sorry, Mr. Gordon. Just as soon as a room is available, I'll get in touch both with her and Dr. Solomon."

The stout man hesitated. "That's your last word on the matter?"

"It's all I'm authorized to do," Rita said carefully. "If you wish to take it up with Dr. Francis, he may decide to make an exception."

"Thank you, Miss Lewis," the angry man said with heavy sarcasm. "You've been very understanding. I won't forget to let Dr. Francis know!" And he turned and strode out to the door, almost colliding with Nurse Laura Graham as he made his exit.

Laura Graham watched after him as he vanished down the hallway, a baffled smile on her worn, motherly face. She was the superintendent of nurses for Riverdale Memorial Hospital and one of the veterans of the staff. She shared a desk in the front office with Rita. Here, just off the lobby, they maintained a liaison between the administrative staff and the various floors. They also had to cope with the demands of doctors and patients' relatives.

"Whatever is wrong with him today?" Laura Graham asked as she came into the room, touching her hand to the nurse's cap perched on her white hair. It was an automatic nervous gesture she repeated often during a conversation.

Rita sighed. "His sister, Mrs. Barry, has been waiting for a room. He thinks she should get it right away."

Laura Graham rolled her eyes. "Mrs. Barry! That's the younger sister who is continually looking for servants. She married that Foster Barry, the lumberman; he's ages older than she. I hear they quarrel all the time."

"Isn't there a story that her father arranged the match?"

Nurse Graham chuckled. "It wouldn't surprise me. Old Morton Gordon would do almost anything for money. And so would Junior. And the weird part of it is they have more than they know what to do with now." She sat at her desk with a sigh.

Rita studied her file again. "I don't know what Dr. Francis will say. But I have an idea he'll send him on his way without giving in to him."

"I almost forgot!" Nurse Graham exclaimed, turning to Rita excitedly. "That boor knocked everything out of my head. I've just come from talking to Winnie at the switchboard. And what do you think?"

Rita gave a resigned smile. "I wouldn't know. So much has been happening in this town lately."

"Well, Riverdale and the town have a new problem on their hands, although they don't know it." Laura Graham bent over, lowering her voice confidentially, "Dr. Francis is leaving!"

"Oh, no!" Rita said. She wasn't the strongest supporter of the debonair, suave young businessman type of doctor who was head of the hospital, but he had done a reasonably good job at a difficult task.

"Winnie overheard the conversation," Laura Graham continued. "He has a good offer from a hospital in Rhode Island, and he plans to hand in his resignation at the board meeting tomorrow night."

"But he can't just walk out until someone

else is found to take his place," Rita protested.

The older nurse shrugged. "He probably plans to stay on until they get someone else," she agreed. "But he'll not let them put him off. He promised that on the phone."

Rita sat back in her chair. "Well, that's really news," she said. "I doubt he'll have much time for Mr. Morton Gordon, Jr.'s problems this afternoon."

Even as she spoke, the phone on her desk rang, and when she picked it up she heard Dr. Charles Francis' easy tones as he spoke from his office down the corridor. "Miss Lewis," he said unctuously, "I understand there's been a slight problem concerning a room for Mr. Gordon's sister."

"I've had a request for a room on file," she said. "None is available, unless she will accept ward accommodation until we can transfer her. I tried to make this clear to Mr. Gordon."

"I see," Dr. Francis said rather unhappily. "Well, that does present a difficulty."

"It does," she agreed, and winked at Laura Graham, who had stopped her work to take it all in.

"What are the prospects for next week?" the superintendent wanted to know.

"Not much better," she said. "Of course

there's always a chance. And I've promised to let Mrs. Barry know."

There was a short pause at the other end of the line, and she could hear the doctor in conversation with the irate Mr. Gordon. She couldn't make out what was being said, but Dr. Francis was speaking in a placating tone.

Then he came on the line again. "Miss Lewis," he began, "if nothing else is available by Monday, I wish you'd allot one of the emergency rooms to Mrs. Barry. She is very anxious to get her stay in hospital over with."

"Yes," Rita said quietly. "I understand she's planning to go abroad."

"Yes," Dr. Francis said, embarrassment plain in his voice. "Thank you, Miss Lewis." And he hung up.

Laura Graham said: "What's the verdict?"

Rita put down the receiver, her blonde attractiveness momentarily marred by a frown. "A compromise in Gordon's favor. If no other room is available by Monday, she gets one of the emergency rooms anyway."

The older nurse gave her a despairing smile. "You know what they say. You can't legislate equality."

"I'm not expecting to in Riverdale," Rita

said bitterly. "This is the kingdom of the Gordons!"

"And the Barrys and the Irwins!" the older nurse prompted with a weary smile. These were the three wealthiest families in the small town; between them they owned nearly all the industry and stores, along with a major portion of the area's real estate.

"It is a sort of Middle Ages situation," Rita agreed. "And those people are the squires."

"Cheer up, peasant," Laura Graham joked. "You're off duty in less than an hour, and this is a good day to go swimming."

"I need something to cool me off," Rita agreed. "Why did I ever come back here? And why do I stay?"

Laura Graham made no attempt to answer those questions as they both settled down to their desk work again. But Rita knew the answers.

She had been born and spent her girlhood in Riverdale. She'd belonged to one of the privileged families in the small New Hampshire town located upstate on the Middlebury River. Her father had owned a small shoe plant, which he'd sold because of ill health, and they'd moved to Florida.

Her father and mother liked the climate and the life, but Rita found herself longing for New England. They were reluctant to have her leave home, but in the end she had convinced them she'd be all right on her own. So they had allowed her to go back to Boston for her nurses' training. She'd completed her three years at an excellent private hospital and stayed on to do general nursing there.

Twice a year she visited her parents in Florida. And during the summer she sometimes spent a week back in Riverdale. It was on one of her visits to Helen Ferguson, a girl friend in her home town, that she renewed her friendship with Cliff Thomson. Cliff had been in her class at school. Later he'd attended Dartmouth, and now he was managing the family furniture business which he'd taken over at the sudden death of his father in a car accident.

Cliff made it plain that he was very fond of her. Even when she went back to Boston he kept in touch with her and visited her frequently. By the end of six months she'd accepted his engagement ring. Meanwhile he began to urge an immediate marriage and complain about them being apart so much of the time.

To put him in a happier frame of mind, she'd left Boston and taken a position with the Riverdale Hospital. She'd not been there

15

a month when Cliff Thomson revealed his true situation to her and let her see why he was so anxious for them to be married. His business was on the verge of bankruptcy. He hoped that when they were married, she would intercede with her father to give him a large loan.

Rita was astounded by his story and thankful that she'd found all this out before their marriage. She made it plain her father no longer had that kind of money and, even if he did have it, she'd be strongly against his granting that kind of favor to Cliff. The young owner of the furniture business was a bluff, jovial ex-football star, and he made a good show of taking her rebuff good-naturedly.

But his ardor cooled. He began to make excuses for not seeing her, and there were no references to marriage plans any more. Rita was in an awkward spot, because in a town such as Riverdale everyone knew everyone else's business, and she was still wearing his engagement ring. However, she decided to stay on, since she'd rented a pleasant cottage near a lake at one end of the town, and she liked her job at the hospital.

The real crisis came about two months later when she came to work one morning to find the hospital seething with excited gossip. At first she couldn't understand why several of the girls shied away from telling her what was going on. Then Winnie, the switchboard operator during the day shift, had called her aside and told her.

"It's Cliff Thomson," she'd said with an animated look on her hatchet face. "He eloped with Sue Irwin last night."

"Sue Irwin!" Rita had exclaimed. Thinking quickly, she could see the logic of it. The Irwins were one of the richest families, and Sue was their eldest and ugliest daughter, a drab creature at least four years older than Cliff. Of course! Cliff had found an answer to his money problems, and Sue Irwin's father would be delighted to see his ugly duckling married.

"It's a rotten trick!" Winnie said with disgust. "Why should he leave a girl like you and marry a frump like Sue Irwin?"

Rita had managed a rueful smile. "It's hard to figure these things out," she said.

"Well, don't you pay any heed to it!" Winnie advised. "Folks in town are all going to be on your side. They'll feel bad for you."

It was the one thing Rita didn't want.

But like most things of this nature, the reality was less embarrassing than her anticipation of it. The hospital staff were particularly considerate of her. And even after Cliff and Sue came back to occupy a fifty-thousand-dollar house in the swank development Irwin money was financing, it didn't make much difference. She had only a casual acquaintance with Sue, and she rarely met the bluff Cliff. When they did meet, he greeted her with boisterous warmth and acted as if all that had happened had been the most natural thing in the world.

She tried to avoid him when she could. Perhaps she shouldn't be so bitter, she thought, but the plain fact was it wasn't so much a matter of bitterness as of her losing all respect for him.

The Irwin furniture business had carried on, and she had heard they'd recently gotten a contract for school furniture that put them in a strong position again. In the last few months the town had started talking about the expensive parties Cliff and Sue were holding for the Riverdale country club crowd.

Naturally Rita had very little to do with this elite circle, although she did attend the country club dances and sometimes went there for dinner with Dr. Paul Reid.

Dr. Reid had come to Riverdale at an excellent time as far as Rita was concerned. He came to take over a retiring physician's practice just after Cliff's elopement with Sue. And his coming served two rather important purposes. A new doctor in town was always a subject for gossip, and this diverted attention from Rita's jilting. Also, he was an excellent young surgeon, and he gave the hospital staff a needed boost.

Rita had liked him from the first moment he presented himself at her desk. "I'm Dr. Reid," he had told her with a smile. "I have a gall bladder coming in. Mrs. Wentworth is the name. I understand you have a semi-private for her on the third floor."

"Yes. We're expecting her this morning," she said. She noted that he had a healthy outdoor look, broad shoulders and a strong face, with a firm chin that indicated character. And he had shining black hair and friendly gray eyes.

"I'm surprised your hospital is so modern," he said.

She smiled. "It's only ten years old. A gift of the Gordon family. They've also endowed it rather heavily."

"I see," he said. "Well, I have nothing against privately endowed hospitals —" he paused, and the gray eyes twinkled — "as long as they operate in the public interest."

Rita was liking him more and more. "We try hard," she said. "The hospital also gets a heavy share of its support from the city council, and the board includes most of the councilmen and the Mayor."

"Sounds nice and democratic," he agreed. "I think I'll get Dr. Francis to let me have a look at your operating room."

"You'll find it good," she said. "We have two. But the larger one has the most up-to-date equipment."

"Thanks," he said. "I'll see you again."

And of course he had. With the passage of the weeks and months, they had become close friends.

Gradually she had found out a good deal concerning Dr. Paul Reid's background. He was from a poor family in the Middle West and had borrowed money and worked as well to pay his way through medical school. To pay back his debt as quickly as possible, he'd taken a commission in the Army. He'd stayed in the service only long enough to satisfy his financial obligations; then he'd been lucky enough to find a position on the staff of a world-famous clinic near his home town. He'd been there until he decided to go into private practice and traveled the long distance to Riverdale.

Again there proved to be a story behind that. He'd spent three years at the Myer Clinic when the head of his department changed. The new man took a strong personal dislike to Paul and this soon led to friction on a professional level. At first Paul couldn't credit his superior's behavior. The reputation of the Myer Clinic was outstanding, and all its medical staff were carefully screened. Yet it was impossible for every weakness of character to be revealed. The man at the head of Paul's department was a petty tyrant, and it didn't take long for the standards of the department to deteriorate.

Paul decided to fight for better conditions and presented a complaint against the department head to the directors of the clinic. Several of the other doctors backed him in his protest and agreed to see the crisis through with him.

But in the end, Paul found himself alone, as the man he opposed put up strong evidence to back his views. It was unfair and was twisted to show Paul in a bad light. His colleagues either said nothing or gave weak testimony that indicated he was the trouble-maker rather than the department head.

Paul had left the service of the Myer Clinic under a shadow. He made up his mind to go into private practice in a small town where he could be entirely his own man. He also wanted to remove himself as far as possible from the scene of his disgrace. So Riverdale had been his choice.

"You two are entirely too quiet!" It was tall Dr. Jonas Arbo who poked his head in the doorway and broke the quiet.

Rita looked up at the veteran general practitioner and smiled. "We're busy finishing up. I'm planning to go to the lake for a swim."

"Excellent idea," the old man said, coming into the office. He was thin, with a lined face, bald and a jovial bedside manner. Popular with the older people in Riverdale, he also had a good reputation as a children's doctor.

Laura Graham smiled at him. They had worked together in Riverdale hospitals for years, first at the old building, and for the last decade in this new one with its hundred and fifty beds.

She said: "It's a wonder you don't retire and do some swimming on your own."

Dr. Jonas Arbo winked. "An idea I've had for some time. Just been putting it off until I can find a female to share my sunset years." He was a widower.

Laura Graham gave Rita a despairing look. "Listen to him!" she said. "And there's not a widow in town hasn't set her cap for him!"

"They don't interest me," he said. "I'm waiting for someone sensible like you."

Laura Graham was a spinster who had a very elderly invalid mother. She gave him a teasing smile. "I don't want a husband. I've got a cat and a dachshund. I'm content."

"A born spinster!" Dr. Jonas Arbo sighed. "I'll just have to keep on waiting and proposing."

The superintendent of nurses changed the subject. "Have you heard about Dr. Francis?"

Dr. Arbo gave her a surprised look. "I thought that was to be strictly secret until the board meeting tomorrow night."

Laura Graham raised her eyebrows. "You know how word gets around, Doctor."

"Indeed I do," he said. "Well, it seems we're going to have to get ourselves another man. Too bad. Francis has been doing well."

Rita joined the conversation. "Maybe the board will make him a better offer and he'll stay on," she suggested.

"Not likely." The tall old doctor shook his head. "Francis has a chance for a larger hospital, and that's what he wants."

Laura Graham said: "Why don't they give you his job?"

"Wouldn't take it," the old man said. "I'm a doctor, not a diplomat. I can't manage my household affairs. What good would I be trying to run a hospital?" He looked at Rita. "Maybe Paul Reid would take it on."

"I don't think so," she said quickly. She was almost sure he wouldn't want it.

"They'll have to look for someone," Dr. Arbo said. "Not too many prospects here in Riverdale except Dr. Solomon, and he's got his practice. And with his asthma, he's not well enough to take on the job of superintendent."

"You brought in Mrs. Crawley," Laura Graham said, referring to one of the veteran doctor's patients. "Have you found out what's wrong with her?"

"Looks like Raynaud's disease," he said. "We've got a nasty situation in her right foot. I'm trying treatments of methacholine chloride. We'll see how she responds."

"That can lead to gangrene, can't it?" Rita asked.

He nodded. "There are small points of it present now."

Laura Graham looked worried. "I warned her she should have seen you ages ago. She complained about her feet and hands going numb, and I noticed they had a bluish tint. But she'd put them in warm water or get some relief and then forget about them until the next time."

"I wish she'd come to me earlier." He sighed. "But we'll do the best we can."

Rita asked: "Is she taking the methacholine chloride by oral dosage or subcutaneous injection?"

Dr. Arbo raised his eyebrows. "You know the injection technique?"

Rita smiled. "I was trained in it when I worked in Boston."

The old man shook his head. "We should have you upstairs instead of down here at a desk. If I remember rightly, you're an anesthetist as well. I have to give Mrs. Crawley the drug orally, because we have neither the equipment necessary nor a trained person to administer it the other way."

"I see," she said. "I suppose you use water and milk to stop the bitter taste."

"Tell me any more," the old man chuckled, "and I'll ask Dr. Francis to transfer you to the case." And with a smile he went on out and down the corridor.

Rita finished her records in time for Miss Cormier, on the relief shift, to take over. She and Laura Graham quickly made their way to the dressing room and changed to their regular clothes. Laura was in a hurry to get home to her mother, and Rita was looking forward to a swim.

Feeling relaxed in a simple yellow dress,

she made her way toward the front entrance of the hospital. She'd almost reached the door when a familiar voice called out her name.

She paused and turned to see Dr. Charles Francis standing at the head of the corridor leading to his office. He motioned to her. "Could I have a minute with you, Miss Lewis?"

Rita walked back to join him, wondering what he had to say to her.

Chapter Two

Dr. Francis led Rita along the corridor to his office and invited her to sit down. Then he closed the door and took his place behind his broad oak desk.

With a polite smile, he said in his precise way: "I'm sorry to detain you on this lovely afternoon, Miss Lewis."

"It's all right," she said.

He sat back with a sigh. "I was sorry to have to interfere in that business of Mrs. Barry. But Gordon was in quite a state."

"I understand."

Dr. Francis smiled apologetically. "One has to consider so many aspects of the situation in a case like this. The most apparent one, Gordon's behavior, was certainly reprehensible. He feels he holds a position of influence and can bring pressure to bear on those of us in charge here. I particularly dislike his attitude when it places people like yourself in a defensive position."

Rita smiled. "I had the advantage of

knowing him and what I might expect his attitude to be."

"And you handled the matter exactly as you should have," the head doctor agreed. "Please don't consider my phone message to you as any sort of reprimand." He paused. "But there is another side to the matter. Although Mrs. Barry is a neurotic daughter of wealth, there is a bare possibility there is more to her migraine condition than any of us are aware of. And because the duty of the hospital is to protect the people of the community, rich and poor, eccentric as well as normal, I hesitate to keep her waiting for a room too long." He gave Rita a sharp look. "Do you follow my thinking, Miss Lewis?"

"Yes, I do, Doctor," she agreed.

Dr. Francis sighed, reached out to his desk and picked up a pencil which he tapped absently on its surface. "Well, that takes care of that," he said. And then: "It's a dark secret, but I'm soon leaving the hospital, Miss Lewis."

"I've heard a rumor," she said. "I'm sorry."

"So am I, in a way." He smiled faintly. "It's a pleasant little town. But it doesn't offer much future for anyone with serious ambitions."

Rita found herself thinking of Paul Reid. He'd given up a career with brilliant possibilities to come to Riverdale. She supposed in a way it had been an acceptance of defeat.

She said: "Have you any idea who might replace you?"

"It will be the main topic of the board meeting tomorrow night," he said. "Are you friendly with Mayor Parent?"

Rita smiled. "I know him very well. I grew up here and know most of the local families. Of course he's about ten years older than I am. He was attending college while I was still in elementary school."

"I see." Dr. Francis nodded. "Then you probably know his cousins, the Grants. They would be older than you and have been away from here for a number of years."

"I do," she told him. At the same time she was wondering what all this might have to do with his successor.

"It happens that one of his cousins is a doctor and qualified for a position of the type I have here," he said. "So the board may not have to look too far to find somebody, since I understand this person is available."

"I didn't know any of the Grant family really well," Rita said. "There were two boys and two girls, and all older, as you say.

But I do know people here liked them. One of the Grants might make a very popular choice."

"Exactly my idea, Miss Lewis." He smiled and stood up. "But don't spread what I've told you around," he said. And as an afterthought: "It's all right to mention it to Dr. Reid if you like."

Rita was also on her feet now, and she felt her cheeks flush. Apparently Dr. Francis had noticed her friendship with his colleague.

The suave little doctor saw her to the door and opened it for her. "Must be pleasant at your cottage these days," he observed.

She smiled. "Yes. It makes up for having to wait for the snow plow in winter."

He nodded. "One disadvantage of living on a side road in this uncertain climate," he agreed.

Rita left the hospital and went directly to her car, which was parked in the area reserved for the staff at the rear of the building.

She passed through the concentrated business district, then past the public library with its pleasant lawn and shade trees, the post office and customs building, and came to the better residential area with fine old mansions set back from the roadway. It was here that the Gordons lived, and the Barrys. The Irwins lived farther out of the town in the new development of Greencrest, about three miles from the city and almost opposite the road where Rita lived; the road leading to the lake.

Rita found the traffic heavy on this sunny afternoon. She passed the entrance to Greencrest with its elaborate pseudo-rustic sign and then had to wait for several cars to pass before she could make the next left turn that led to her road.

She slowed her speed as she approached her own driveway. Jumping out of the car quickly, she ran up the several steps of her verandah and unlocked the door of the rather plain, story-and-a-half white house. The mailman had been by and taken the trouble to get out of his car and push her letters through the metal slot in the front door. She had a box on a post near the road, and all he was expected to do was put her mail in that. But during the summer months he gave her this special service.

She scanned the letters quickly, discarding a couple of bills and a letter soliciting her subscription to a magazine. What was left was a card from one of the nurses at the hospital who was visiting Europe.

Having gone over her mail, Rita quickly

changed to her bathing suit. She found towels, her beach bag with cap, sun lotion and other needed paraphernalia. Then she put on her dark sun glasses again and got into the car to drive the short distance to the lake.

A few minutes later she arrived at the parking place cleared from the woods area by the residents of the road and saw there was only one other car there. It belonged to a young couple who lived near the main road and had three young children. She imagined their mother had brought them down to enjoy the water. No doubt others had been there earlier, and some would come down after husbands had returned from work. Helen Ferguson usually waited for Bill, and sometimes they had a picnic on the beach instead of dinner at home.

She left her car and walked the short distance to the beach. The woman with the three youngsters had taken a place far down to the left. Seeing Rita, she waved but made no attempt to join her. The children were noisy and active, and she no doubt preferred to cope with them on her own.

Rita slipped on her bathing cap, put down the towels, blanket and bag, and made her way down the beach and into the refreshing water of the lake. It wasn't cold, or even cool. But it was pleasantly warm, and as she went farther out the temperature of the water seemed just right after the hot hours at her desk.

Later, she stretched out on the blanket and closed her eyes to enjoy the sun. She must have dropped off to sleep, for with a sense of surprise she became conscious of someone walking near her. Quickly raising herself on an elbow, she looked around to see Cliff Thomson standing smiling down at her.

"Hardly recognized you in the dark glasses," he said. "Wouldn't have thought about you being here except that I saw your car."

Rita sat up. "Aren't you a long way from your office?" she asked.

His broad face took on a smile. "I have the afternoon off." His hair was light brown and crew cut.

"Lucky you," she said without enthusiasm.

"How about yourself?" he challenged her in his usual hearty way.

"I worked until an hour ago," she reminded him. "I'm on the seven to three shift."

He nodded. "Sure! I forgot those crazy hospital hours." He gazed out at the lake, still making no move to go. Rita found herself angered and embarrassed by his intrusion.

"I'm going to put a boat on the lake," he told her.

"Oh!" She let him know it was a matter of complete disinterest to her.

"Yeah!" he said importantly. "I'm tired of the river. It's getting too crowded. I'm buying a lot on the lake and building me a little dock."

Rita glanced up at him as he studied the lake with narrowed eyes, an expression of ownership already on his arrogant, coarsely good-looking face. Yes, she thought with a sigh, he's already planning to be the bully of the lake. And for perhaps the hundredth time she wondered what she had ever seen in him.

She thought she'd give him something to worry about. "It will soon be as bad here as it is on the river," she warned. "They come on weekends and bring their boats on top of their cars and on trailers. They don't worry about wharves or private property. There's nothing you can do about it."

Cliff looked at her darkly. "You've never forgiven me for marrying Sue," he said. "You want to keep a feud going!"

Rita managed to keep her voice in control

and her face expressionless. "Do you think it's good taste to bring that up?"

"Who worries about good taste?" he snapped. "I thought a lot of you, Rita. I still do, for that matter. I was in a spot and you wouldn't try to help me. I had to bail myself out."

"Well, let's forget it," she said. "It's worked out very well for you."

He studied her angrily. "All right; I don't love Sue. But she did get me out of my trouble. Now I'm riding high. And we could do things for you. See you get around with the right crowd!"

"I'm doing very well on my own, thank you," Rita said coldly, and turned away from him.

But he still continued in his urgent, sullen tone. "The medical aristocracy? They don't count much in this town. You can do better than Paul Reid!"

Rita dug furiously in the sand with the fingers of her right hand. "Please, will you go," she said, "if you're any kind of a gentleman!"

"I'm your friend, Rita," he argued. "And I could be an even better friend if you'd let me. You and that doctor of yours avoid Sue and me at the club. You're not going to get anywhere running off to corners when we show up. Sue and I could have you to our place, get you in with the real people."

With a last patient effort she turned to him wearily. "Cliff, are you going to leave me alone, or do I have to get off the beach?"

He stared at her a moment in his overbearing way. "Okay," he said. "Have it your way! But you're making a bad mistake. I want to be friends."

She said: "Surely you can best prove your friendship by leaving me alone."

"You want folks to keep on talking," he said. "Best way to manage that is to go around not speaking to each other. If they see we're friends, they'll forget all the old stuff."

Rita looked up at him. "I'm willing to speak to you, as long as you're enough of a gentleman to keep your place and move on."

"But you don't want to be friends?"

"I like the privilege of choosing my friends," she said.

He gave a bitter laugh. "Maybe you'll change your mind one of these days. If you do, I'll be glad to meet you more than halfway."

"If you do, bring a boat here," she said. "Remember what I've told you. We speak, and that's all."

"Sure, I'll remember," he said. "See you

around." And he walked leisurely back to the parking lot. Only when she heard the motor of his car start and the sound of it driving away did she lose some of her tenseness.

She stayed on the beach for another half-hour, then drove back to the cottage and prepared her dinner. She was expecting Dr. Paul Reid to come down for the evening, but he had office hours from six-thirty until eight, so it wasn't likely she'd see him until nine.

Dinner consisted of a salad and iced tea. Then she sat to read for a while before dressing for Paul's arrival. She'd not been on the verandah for more than five minutes when Helen Ferguson drove up in her station wagon. She was alone except for Spotty, who sat proudly on the front seat beside her.

Rita got up and gave her friend a smile of greeting and Spotty, who was already up the steps and on the verandah frantically wagging his tail, a friendly pat on the head.

"Hope I'm not bothering you," Helen said. She was a blonde like Rita, but darker and tending to plumpness. The print sun suit she still wore revealed this.

"No. I'm just taking a few minutes before I dress for the evening," she said, and waved for her friend to sit on the wicker seat beside her.

Helen plumped down with a sigh and, stretching out her legs, regarded her dimpled knees. "I'm really getting fat," she said.

Rita smiled. "I wouldn't consider your problem serious," she said.

Helen looked at her with a grimace. "Well, the summer is just beginning," she said. "And by the time I chase the girls around in this heat for another few months, I'll probably be back to normal."

"That's a healthy outlook," Rita agreed.

Helen gave her a look of interest. "While I think of it," she said, "didn't I see someone you know drive down to the beach this afternoon just a little while after you did?"

"Cliff Thomson?"

"I thought it was him!"

"Don't get ideas," Rita warned her friend. "His being there was as much a surprise to me as it was to you. In fact, it was more an unhappy experience than a surprise."

Helen's eyes widened. "Were you actually talking to him?"

"He came over and started a conversation."

"He has a nerve," her friend said indignantly. "What could he possibly have to say you'd want to hear?"

"He broke the good news he's buying a lakefront lot and bringing a boat down here," Rita said with a sigh.

"But that's terrible," Helen said. "What will you do?"

"Avoid him whenever I can," Rita smiled. "He can't be there every minute of every day." She tried to sound more hopeful about the situation than she actually felt.

Helen commiserated: "Still it won't be the same."

"There's not much you can do about it," Rita said. "I see him at the country club when we go there. Of course Paul is always with me."

"And that makes a difference," Helen agreed. Then, changing the subject: "Rita, I came over for Bill. He wants to know if you have any more of those little yellow pain pills?"

Rita hesitated a moment. Paul had given her a supply of the pills when she'd given an ankle a bad sprain that had bothered her for weeks. They were fairly strong and not available without prescription.

One evening when she'd been at the Fergusons', Helen's husband had complained about his back. As Rita understood it, he had been in a bad auto accident on the West Coast before coming to Riverdale, and his back had given him trouble ever since. The accident had happened seven or eight years before, but he still had periods when the pain was severe.

Wanting to help in an emergency, she'd gone back to the cottage and gotten a few of the tablets for him. Later he had asked for more. And now he had again sent Helen over for some.

Rita gave her friend a worried glance. "Is his back acting up again?"

Helen nodded. "He's been pacing back and forth ever since dinner."

"He should see a doctor. Do you want me to ask Paul to drop over after he gets here?"

"No, please don't do that," Helen said. "You know how peculiar he is. He gets really upset when I mention doctors."

"But if his back is as bad as you say —"

"I know," Helen interrupted with a sigh. "And I agree. I'm trying to get him to come around to the idea. Meanwhile, if you have the pills, they would help."

Rita got up. "I may have a few left. There can't be many."

"We don't want to rob you," Helen said, but she followed Rita into the house.

Rita went to the medicine cabinet and brought down the small plastic container with the half-dozen yellow tablets left in it.

She handed the vial to Helen. "You may as well take them all," she said.

"You're sure it's all right?" Helen asked, but she took the vial at once.

Rita nodded. "If I need them again, Paul will let me have them." She saw Helen out to the verandah again. "But you must talk to Bill. If he doesn't get better right away, you should force him to see a doctor."

"I'll talk to him tonight," Helen said unhappily. "And I'll let him know these are the last of your tablets. That may make up his mind."

"But it's so silly for him to put off seeing a doctor," Rita said. "He may find himself off his feet altogether. Lately I've hated to ask him to come over and do anything for me. He hasn't looked well."

"He's well enough." Helen smiled. "It's just that he gets these attacks. One thing about it: they don't last!"

"What sort of back injury did he get in that car crash?" Rita asked, as she followed her friend down the verandah steps and out to the station wagon.

Helen let the dog jump into the front seat first. She turned to Rita. "You know how mysterious men like to be! He hardly ever talks about his life in California. And he's never really told me what they had to do for his back. I do know he was in hospital for a long while."

"See if you can get him to talk to Paul about it," Rita said. "I expect we'll be here all evening. And Paul wouldn't mind."

"I'll ask him," Helen said, getting behind the wheel and closing the door. "But don't wait around for a call. I can't see him agreeing. Anyway, the tablets will help him."

Rita waited until her friend had backed out the driveway and was on the main road. She waved goodbye and waited until the station wagon was out of sight. Then she turned back toward the house.

Chapter Three

It was the season of long, light evenings, and when Dr. Paul Reid wheeled his car into the driveway behind Rita's at a little after nine there was still no trace of dusk.

He bounded lightly up the verandah stairs, and she met him at the door with a smile. Paul threw himself on the wicker settee with a big sigh.

"It's good to sit a few minutes in the air again," he said. "I thought I'd never get the office emptied tonight."

"I thought you were later than usual," she said, standing by him. "Would you like something cold?"

He nodded. "The regular."

She went inside to prepare his drink. As she busied herself, she called out: "I went down to the beach for a while this afternoon."

"Lucky you," he said.

"Not as lucky as you think," she called back. And then she pushed the screen door open and came back with his glass. She'd also prepared a tall, cooling drink for herself, and now she sat on the verandah railing facing him.

"I suppose a lot of thirst is purely mental," he said with a grin on his rugged young face. "But on a warm night like this a cold drink helps."

"Any interesting cases?" she asked.

"Mostly the regulars," he said. "It always saddens me that people born with weak, ailing bodies continue all through life with the idea that some doctor can give them new ones."

Rita had heard him complain about this before. She gave him an amused look. "I suppose they have to have something to hope for."

Paul took another sip of his drink. "Not that they have shorter lives than the rest of us," he said. "At least the majority of them don't. They often outlive their healthy relatives. But they can't believe that this dull, aching shell is the only one they'll ever have and as perfect as it will ever be."

"You must admit medicine can relieve some of the minor discomfort."

"Agreed," he said. "And that's the sort of people that keep general practitioners like me in business." He shook his head. "I almost wish I'd found myself another research job."

Rita took hold of the verandah post with her free hand. "A few months ago you weren't talking that way," she said with a laugh.

"A few months ago I was as naïve as a child," he told her. "Now I see you can't avoid playing politics, no matter what you do or where you go. You can't avoid dealing with people, and as long as you have to do that, it's wise to be prepared for deception and disillusionment."

She sipped the cool liquid in her glass. "You have had a bad evening!"

"And of course there were the usual summer problems! Poison ivy! A whole family in a mess because the male parent, who'd never been away from Brooklyn before, decided he was a born naturalist. Stomach upsets in a couple from the hotel who couldn't resist overloading because the food was good and unlimited there. And three cases of severe sunburn because the youngster driving his first new convertible forgot that his skin and that of the girls with him wasn't fine Morocco leather. They drove five hundred miles with the top down in a blazing sun and expected me to give them some wonder cure

45

that would clear up their burns in ten minutes."

"Doctor, you have my sympathy," she said with mock solemnity.

He finished his drink and put the glass down on the verandah floor near his feet. Then he stared disgustedly at the lawn. "All those years of toil and dedication to acquire a minimum of skill, and when I try to put it to some use, I have to squander it on a choice collection of human stupidities!"

"Surely you had at least one patient tonight who made you feel your M.D. wasn't wasted."

Paul smiled at her. "I had a couple, as a matter of fact. One was a middle-aged man with what I think is a peptic ulcer. He's had the usual pain, the gnawing, burning type. Some nausea, but still maintains a decent appetite."

She nodded agreement. "Sounds like the pattern."

"I'm almost sure of it," he said. "I'm arranging for an X-ray examination and possible hospitalization if necessary. I think we've caught the condition before it has gone too far, and drug therapy will take care of it."

"For a surgeon you're very anxious not to use the knife."

"Most surgeons who are worth their salt avoid an operation when it isn't required," Paul said seriously. "At the same time they don't dodge one when it is, no matter how hopeless the outlook seems."

"What was your other interesting case tonight?"

"A girl with dermatitis of the auricle and external ear canal," he said. "A bad case. She has a history of anemia, and I'd say this was a side problem. In any case, her ear canal was blistered and in bad shape. It will take some time to make any headway with it."

"Cortisone and an antibiotic, I suppose?" Rita said, suggesting a treatment she'd seen used.

"Some kind of combination of that type," he agreed, "plus a lot of patience on her part and mine." He paused. "I've been doing all the complaining. You should have a turn. What about your day?"

Rita grimaced. "Mine was really something. I had a run-in with Morton Gordon, Jr. for a start."

"Some start!" Paul said with sympathy. "What was that all about? I thought he kept clear of the hospital except at board meetings."

"He does usually. But his sister, Mrs.

47

Barry, has had trouble getting a room." And she went on to explain the details.

Paul chuckled. "I must tease Dr. Solomon about that in the morning."

Rita sighed and with forced casualness stared out at the lawn. "Then when I came home to recuperate with a swim and a rest afterward on the beach, I was bothered by my old boy friend."

"Cliff Thomson!" Paul sounded surprised.

She faced him with a smile. "None other."

The young doctor frowned. "He has some nerve! I've noticed him trying to get your attention at the club. You'd think he'd have the decency to mind his own business."

"If Cliff has any principles, he's happily unaware of them."

"What did you do?"

She shrugged and looked down at the empty glass which she held in her hands. "I asked him to leave. He became highly upset and informed me he was buying land on the lake and doing some boating here."

"That's great news!" Paul said in disgust. "It's a wonder he didn't want to drain it and move it closer to Greencrest."

"After a while he drove away," she said. And she joined Paul on the settee. "So you see my day wasn't all peaches and cream, either."

Paul slipped his arm around her and drew her close to him. She relaxed with her head on his shoulder, conscious of the regular rise and fall of his breathing. She felt his lips brush her hair, and then he cupped her chin in his hand and turned her face so he could kiss her properly.

When he drew away, he had a touch of anger in his face. "One of these days I'm going to punch the living daylights out of the magnificent Cliff Thomson," he said.

She looked at the boyish rage in his face with loving eyes and laughing softly. "How would that kind of a fist fight fit in with the picture of the sober young doctor?"

"I have a limit," he said grimly. "Thomson had better leave you alone."

"I can handle him, darling," she promised.

"Not if he's around here all the time, as he will be if he starts using the lake," Paul worried. "I don't like the sound of that at all."

"Don't waste your worry," she cautioned. "We'll wait and see if it really happens."

The evening was now on the edge of darkness. Paul tightened the pressure of his arm about her protectively. "We could avoid all this if you'd marry me right away as I want you to."

"Let the old scandal die down before we create a new one," she said in a weary voice.

"Marrying me wouldn't create a scandal!" Paul protested.

"I didn't mean exactly that," she said. "But it would cause talk. Let's wait until the end of the year, anyway."

"And have Thomson bothering you all summer," he said angrily. "I'll bet he has his eye on you again. Probably thinks you're putting up a brave front, but underneath you're still madly in love with him."

"He is that egotistic," she admitted. "And he did actually say he wasn't in love with Sue!"

"That's a gallant statement if I ever heard one," Paul stormed. "He sure was infatuated with her money. That's the kind of husband material I'd like to take care of with some nice toxic drug."

"There's a law against poisoning, dear," she reminded him.

"Oughtn't to be in cases like Thomson's," he said. "There's going to be a moon. Let's go for a drive and forget him."

She knew he enjoyed driving. "All right," she said. "I'll put these glasses inside and lock up."

She locked the door and put her sweater over her arm, and they went down to his car.

They usually drove to Scarboro and had a snack at the restaurant and got back before midnight. Rita didn't like to be out too late, as she got up early in the morning to be at the hospital by seven.

There was a ten-mile stretch along the river between Riverdale and Scarboro. Here there were fewer houses, and most of them were owned by the wealthy in the two cities. The promised moon was now reflected in silver on the broad river, and Paul called Rita's attention to it.

"That alone is worth the drive," he said.

Rita stared out at the lovely view. "I agree," she said.

Paul glanced at her with a smile. "I wish some of the so-called artists we have in Riverdale would try their hand at that scene instead of the weird subjects I saw at the spring show."

"You don't approve of their abstracts?" she asked with a laugh.

"I prefer the river as we're seeing it now to a lot of red, white and blue cubes with an arrow stuck in them or a close-up view of the bottom of three ugly feet!"

"It's not the art that upset you," she said. "It's the clinical fact that no one has three feet! I remember you raged for hours after we went to the show."

"Let someone do the river by moonlight and I'll put my money on the line," he told her. "I have just the place in my office to hang it: on the wall across from my desk. And when things get bad, I can always look over the patient's shoulder and relax!"

Rita was going to make a reply, but as they rounded a curve a waving light ahead caught her attention. "What's that?" she asked.

Paul slowed the car. "Looks like a state trooper," he said. And then: "See, there's his car to the side, with the red beacon blinking."

They pulled up to the shoulder and parked a few feet from the policeman with the signal flashlight. Paul left the parking lights on and jumped out of the car, with Rita close behind him.

Traffic was being halted both ways. There was a policeman farther up the road blocking the other lane. And now Rita saw what had happened. One car was overturned in the ditch to the left, and the other, badly smashed, was crossways on the left lane. She saw a body stretched out on the asphalt by the car, a blanket spread over it.

Paul questioned the state trooper. "Have you got an ambulance on the way?"

The young officer nodded grimly. "We're waiting for one from Riverdale now."

"I'm a surgeon from Riverdale," Paul told him. "And this young woman is a nurse. Can we help?"

The state trooper gave him a relieved look. "You sure can, mister," he said. "Come with me." He led them to the blanket-covered body. "Just the driver in the other car, and he's done for. This one was alive when I checked last. There's a younger man still in the front seat. We didn't dare move him."

Paul bent over the body and lifted the blanket. Rita had an immediate impulse to turn away when she saw the accident victim's badly battered head. But she forced herself to kneel by Paul.

He shook his head. "He's gone now," he said, and put the blanket back over the body.

The state trooper shook his head. "I've got to get back to my station until we get some help here," he said. "Take a look at the one on the front seat."

Paul and Rita made their way to the damaged car. The doors were sprung open, and the front of the vehicle completely wrecked. A crowd of spectators, mostly drivers from the halted line of cars that now stretched for some distance, was gathered around the wreck.

"I'm a doctor," Paul announced, pushing his way through. The people quickly stepped back, allowing them to reach the injured man.

Rita stood by as Paul again made a quick examination of the body laid out on the broad seat. She could see he'd been badly injured. There was a gash at his temple and a cut across his cheek.

"How is he?" she asked.

Paul spoke grimly without looking up from his examination. "He's alive," he said. "The head injuries seem minor. It's the chest damage that looks the worst. He's badly crushed on the right side. Internal hemorrhage, and who knows what other complications."

Rita asked: "Is there anything I can do?"

"Nothing anyone can do until we get him on an operating table," Paul said, looking up at her. "He needs surgery, and fast!" He glanced around. "It's taking that ambulance long enough."

"There's no regular driver on duty at night," she reminded him. "They've probably had to locate him."

Paul glanced at her sharply. "I didn't know that."

"One of the general maintenance men acts as driver after seven," she said.

Paul again turned toward the motionless figure stretched out on the front seat. "This man will probably die before the ambulance gets here."

"Oh, no!" she said.

He made no answer but roughly pushed his way through the crowd and made a line for the state trooper. The crowd closed their tight circle around the wrecked car again, and Rita could hear the low murmur of their questions.

Glancing down at the wan face of the man on the car seat, the closed eyes, the vivid streaks of crimson on the left side of his face, she felt a sense of panic and frustration. With reluctance she forced herself to take the limp wrist of the prostrate figure before her and feel for a sign of a pulse.

Her panic grew when she found none. She raised her head and saw Paul striding quickly back. "I think he's gone," she said, as the young doctor came up to her.

Paul bent quickly over the figure again. This time quite a period elapsed before he looked up. "You're right," he said at last. "He's gone."

Almost as the words escaped his mouth, the shrill sound of the ambulance siren filled the night air as it approached from the direction of Riverdale.

The young doctor gave her a bitter look. "There's no hurry now," he said. "The undertaker won't be in a rush."

She studied his angry young face with worried eyes. "It wouldn't have made any difference," she said. "Even if the ambulance had gotten here earlier, he'd undoubtedly have died on the way to the hospital."

"He'd at least have had a chance," Paul said. "Now he's dead because somebody found a way to nick a few dollars off the hospital budget."

Rita made no answer. But she knew that Paul would be having something to say to Dr. Francis tomorrow. She only hoped he wouldn't involve himself in another hopeless battle. The ambulance drew up, with a screeching of tires, and they stepped back.

Chapter Four

Rita awoke the next morning feeling tired and with a trace of a headache. Paul had driven her home directly after the accident. Neither of them had felt like going anywhere. She had persuaded him to come in for coffee, and all during the time he stayed he continued to storm about the laxity that had caused the ambulance to arrive at the accident scene so late.

Sleep eluded her when she went to bed. She found herself tossing and turning restlessly long after she'd turned out the light.

At last she fell asleep from sheer exhaustion. But when the alarm rang and she reached out sleepily to turn it off, she felt as if she hadn't really gotten any rest at all.

It was another bright summer day, and again a busy one at Riverdale Memorial Hospital. Arriving at her desk, Rita made a thorough check of patients being admitted that day and also those who would be receiving their discharge. It was one of those days when there would be many changes.

Not an hour after she began work, Dr. Solomon arrived with the first problem of the morning. He was one of the senior doctors and highly respected by both the hospital staff and the community. A slightly stooped man with a long, doleful face and iron gray hair, he was an expert in the field of internal medicine. He had heavy eyelids and a rather hesitant manner, but they disguised great alertness of mind. He invariably summer and winter wore a tweed suit of mixed brown pattern, and it was a joke among the staff that he never changed it but took it off when he was called to the operating room as an observer and then had it pressed to use again. The truth was he'd found this type of suit serviceable, and as one wore out he bought another.

Now he came into the office in his usual unhurried, cautious manner, his head slightly to one side as he nodded to Rita and said: "Miss Lewis, I need your cooperation in an emergency."

She smiled at him, because she knew he never asked favors unless there was a good reason. Dr. Solomon was not one to impose. She said: "Anything I can manage."

"I need a private room at once," he said with a sigh. "Difficult situation! Extremely difficult! The girl is outside in the business office now, going through the usual red tape. I thought I'd speak to you about her admittance and get it speeded up if possible."

Rita put her list of admissions for the day before her on the desk. "Is she listed?"

The long, doleful face took on an even more woebegone expression. He made an impatient gesture. "No, no, that's the whole point! I really must have a room for her at once. She's a very sick girl, a leukemia case. I've treated her before, and now she's had an alarming relapse."

Rita glanced at her list. "I can find a room for her," she said. "On the third floor, 318."

The old doctor nodded solemnly. "Thank you, Miss Lewis. I knew you'd help if you could. This is an extremely sad case. The girl's widowed mother lives near here, but she can't give her daughter much attention because of an arthritic condition of her own. The girl has been living in Portsmouth. Her husband is a captain in one of the new atomic submarines. He only has short periods of leave. Naturally, her condition is a great strain on him."

"Naturally."

"He's due to report back to Portsmouth

later today," Dr. Solomon continued. "They're doing testing on a new sub. He felt she would be better here with me, since I've treated her before. And she is handier to her mother."

"Has she had the condition long?" Rita asked.

"She's going into her second year with it," he said. He shook his head. "I've tried radio-active phosphorus, and she seemed to do well. Now it's either to be Fowler's solution or a new drug I've had sent down from Sloane-Kettering. She's a lovely girl; it saddens me to have to hospitalize her again. But she's had a severe regression. She's very weak."

"I'll call the floor supervisor on three," Rita promised. "She'll be expecting you. As soon as she's finished with the office, take her on up."

"Fine." The old doctor started for the door and then turned with an apologetic lift of his hand. "Dear me, I forgot an important item. Her name is Grace Thomas; Mrs. Jack Thomas, to be exact."

Rita nodded. "Thank you, Doctor."

She put through the call to the third floor and made arrangements for the girl's room. Then she gave her attention to some routine paper work.

Laura Graham came bustling in. "Things are really humming around here today," she said. And as she seated herself at her desk, she glanced across at Rita with a confidential air.

"You know I think half the hospital knows Dr. Francis is going," she said. "It seems to be anything but a well kept secret."

Rita laughed. "Probably everyone has passed the word along to everybody else that it's strictly confidential."

"Well, they're all talking! I'll bet that board meeting tonight will be a warm one."

"Dr. Reid is operating this morning, isn't he?" Rita asked the superintendent of nurses.

Laura Graham nodded. "He and Dr. Arbo are doing a gall bladder. And then I believe Dr. Reid has an appendectomy." She glanced at the clock. "I imagine he's probably finished by now."

Rita briefly told the other nurse about the incident of the previous night. Laura Graham listened to her with a troubled expression on her pale, lined face. The older woman seemed shocked by the story.

"What a dreadful thing!" she observed when Rita had finished. "That Fowler is never around when you want him."

"He's the maintenance man you spoke of,

isn't he?" Rita said. "You had a lot of trouble with him."

"Anything you ask him to do is a burden," Laura Graham said angrily. "No matter what it might be he complains. And he takes twice the time anyone else would."

"Why do they keep him on?"

The white-haired nurse shrugged. "The pay isn't marvelous, and hospital help is hard to get these days."

They paused in their conversation as a shy-looking young man in naval uniform paused in the doorway. He was tall, dark and had a round boyish face. Just now he looked worried.

"I'm sorry to interrupt," he said, and Rita noted that he had a Southern drawl.

Rita smiled. "That's quite all right. Please come in."

The young man advanced hesitantly. "I'm Captain Thomas. I want to thank you for helping the doctor get my wife a room right away. She's getting settled in it now."

Rita studied the young man with sympathetic eyes. He couldn't be more than twenty-five.

"It's my job," she said. "But I do appreciate your coming by to thank me."

Captain Thomas fingered his gold-braided cap nervously. "I've been to a few hospitals before, and the red tape can snarl you up some. Grace isn't well enough to stand too much waiting around these days."

"I'm sorry," she said quietly.

The young naval officer attempted a smile. "Well, at least she's in good hands." He looked at them both anxiously. "Dr. Solomon is a good doctor?"

Laura Graham gave him a motherly smile. "I don't know who I'd rather have looking after me than Dr. Solomon," she said. And then, by way of changing the subject: "What branch of the service are you in, Captain?"

He smiled. "I'm a junior officer in the submarine service," he said. "We're testing the new atomic models they're building in Portsmouth."

The senior nurse showed interest. "Of course. I've read about them. But I always forget how handy Portsmouth is. I'm afraid my world is pretty well confined to the hospital walls."

"We all tend to become that way," he agreed. "I don't have much knowledge about anything but my job." He nodded to Rita again. "I won't keep you back any longer. Thank you again." And he strode out.

When he had gone, Laura Graham turned to Rita. "What's his story?"

"His wife has leukemia," Rita said. "Dr.

Solomon has been treating her for more than a year. He doesn't seem hopeful."

The older nurse's face took on a sad look. "I should think not," she said. "The poor thing is lucky to have lived this long." She sighed. "What a shame!"

"They're both so young," Rita agreed.

"That's the tragedy of it," Laura Graham said. "Death can be a blessing when it comes at the right time. It would be now for my mother. Poor dear, last night she was very bad. And yet she just can't seem to go." She paused as if considering. "Then you hear of a case like this. It makes you wonder." With a troubled sigh, she returned to her work.

Rita had several phone calls in rapid succession, and each of them brought a small problem to be attended to. Before she knew it, the clock on the wall facing her desk showed eleven. She hadn't even taken a coffee break, and she was beginning to feel hungry and a little weary. But she went to lunch at twelve, so she decided to work on until then.

She was bent over her typewriter when she heard familiar footsteps and lifted her head with a smile. As she expected, it was Dr. Paul Reid. He seemed to show no ill effects from the night before or his busy morning session at the operating table.

64

He nodded to her brusquely as he would have to a stranger. "I wonder if Miss Graham could cover for you a few minutes?" he asked. "I'd like to have you come in to see Dr. Francis with me."

An instant look of apprehension came into Rita's eyes. She said: "Do you think it's really necessary?"

Paul nodded. "I've been talking to him. But he'd like to have you corroborate some of the details."

Rita glanced at Laura Graham. "Will you take over for me?"

The older woman smiled. "Any time. Go ahead."

As she walked with Paul along the corridor that led to Dr. Francis' office, she said in a low voice: "You've really started the ball rolling."

He kept his eyes ahead, his face stern. "You knew I would, didn't you?"

"I was afraid so after last night."

He gave her a sharp glance. "Don't you think I'm in the right?"

"Of course, darling," she said in the same low voice. "But you can't expect much action from Dr. Francis at a time like this. All he's thinking of is getting away from here."

"We'll give him something else to consider, for variety's sake," Paul said firmly.

Paul stood aside so she could enter the superintendent's office first. Her immediate impression was that Dr. Francis was something less than happy to see them. But he met the situation bravely, rose with a polite smile on his narrow face and waved her to a chair.

"We're beginning to see a lot of each other, Miss Lewis," he said with just a trace of sarcasm in his tone.

"I'm afraid so," she said quietly as she sat down.

Paul and Dr. Francis both remained standing. The little doctor studied her from behind his desk. "From what Dr. Reid has told me, the ambulance was extremely slow arriving at the accident scene last night."

"It did seem a long time," she said.

Paul spoke up angrily. "I'd say a good twenty-five minutes was lost, and that could have meant the difference between life and death for the patient we found alive when we arrived on the scene."

"A very bad business," Dr. Francis said with a frown. "And you're quite certain the delay had nothing to do with heavy traffic or any other type of road condition?"

Paul shook his head. "I've checked that through with the state police. As a matter of record, the ambulance had a police car with it all the way from the Riverdale city limits, giving it clearance."

"Then the delay really did occur at the hospital?" the other doctor said.

"It did," Paul agreed. "And when I questioned this Fowler about having taken so long, he was rude in his replies. He showed no regrets and was in a plainly antagonistic mood."

"You heard him, I suppose, Miss Graham?" Dr. Francis gave her a keen look.

She nodded. "Yes. I couldn't help overhearing the conversation. Fowler behaved badly, and his replies to Dr. Reid's questions were very unsatisfactory. I'd call them inflammatory."

"I see." Dr. Francis showed that the gravity of the situation was not lost on him. "I've called Fowler and asked him to report here," he said. "He's off duty at this time of day, but he should get here during the noon hour period. I'll interview him as soon as he comes."

"I've asked some questions," Paul said. "It seems he removed a portable air-conditioning unit that wasn't working properly from the diet kitchen. He needed some sort of part. Instead of waiting until morning and sending for the part then, he left the hospital in his own car and went to a friend's workshop to get what he needed. It was while he was gone the call for the ambulance came in. No one knew where he was until he drove up by the rear entrance. Then someone told him, and he went directly to the ambulance." He paused, with a bitter expression on his rugged young face. "Naturally, by that time it was too late."

"And he had no authority to leave the building?" Dr. Francis questioned.

"His own," Paul said with irony.

"I'll talk to him," Dr. Francis promised. "And naturally, this will have to be brought to the attention of the board this evening." He paused. "I'm not too much in favor of our present system, nor have I any excuse to offer for Fowler's behavior. The entire business must be threshed out thoroughly." Dr. Francis gave Paul a meaningful look. "I don't know if we'll come up with anything better or not. The ambulance system is a problem for most hospitals. And it's a scandal in the great cities like New York and Chicago. But we can present the matter and make a try."

"I can't see how we can ignore what's happened," Paul said firmly.

"Believe me, I have no intention of doing so," Dr. Francis said in his precise way. "Although after this evening's meeting my position will be somewhat altered here, I'll still be in charge until I leave."

"I understand that, sir," Paul said.

"Of course I'll want you to attend the meeting," Dr. Francis said. "I'm afraid it may be a lengthy one, but I'll try to see you make your appearance before the board as early in the evening as possible."

"It will be all right," Paul said. "I have no office hours this evening."

"Then we'll consider it settled," Dr. Francis said, and turned to Rita. "I don't think it will be necessary for you to attend, Miss Lewis. I will take the liberty of mentioning that you were present and the gist of what you've told me."

"Anything that will help," she agreed.

"Fine." The superintendent nodded. "Thank you both for giving me your cooperation. I'll interview Fowler when he comes and try to get this prepared for the board later."

They left after a moment, and Rita felt some relief at having the interview over with. She glanced at Paul as they went back along the corridor and thought he also looked less strained.

"What do you think?" she asked.

He gave her a cynical glance. "I don't count on anything until I see results. Tonight's meeting will give me a better idea of what good we may have accomplished," he said.

They had come to the end of the corridor, and now they stood for a moment before parting company. Rita didn't know quite what to say to this man she loved and wanted to protect. A direct warning might be misunderstood and annoy him. All she could do was give him a hint that caution was desirable.

She looked up at him with a faint smile. "You won't try to topple the foundations of the hospital with one blow tonight?"

Paul's eyes narrowed slightly. "Just what does that mean?"

"You won't rush in with both arms swinging?" she went on. "In the end, you can accomplish just as much by tact."

He laughed lightly. "You're afraid I'm going to wind up in a brawl."

"Lately you've been showing a tendency to look for one," she warned. "Don't spoil your chances for doing good here by hasty words or action." This was a lot more direct than she'd intended, but the words came spontaneously.

For a moment she was certain the young doctor was going to take offense. But he said: "Don't worry about it." He glanced at his wristwatch. "It's almost noon, and I've hardly made a start on my rounds yet." With a parting nod, he headed for the elevator and the upstairs floors.

Chapter Five

Rita had just gotten back from lunching in the cafeteria when Dr. Jonas Arbo's spare figure appeared in the doorway. The thin old doctor had a look of grim humor on his lined face.

"I hope you had a good lunch, Miss Lewis," he said, coming up to her desk.

"Excellent, thank you, Doctor," she said.

He rubbed a hand along the side of his neck and looked sheepish. "Well, at least that gets us off to a good start," he said. "I'm afraid that a small problem has developed."

"Oh?" Rita smiled faintly.

The thin man leaned forward confidentially, his hands resting on the edge of her desk. "The business office has messed things up for a patient of mine."

"In what way?"

"Well, unless we have two rooms numbered 227, my patient has been called in on the wrong day," he said. "I have Mrs. Galway, a diabetic, waiting out in the lobby.

She was called by the business office to come, and she's here. But there happens to be a patient in 227 already."

Rita consulted her chart. "Of course there is." And she ran her eye down the admissions list. "Mrs. Galway should have been called on Saturday. She's two days early."

Dr. Jonas Arbo straightened up with a small groan. "That's just dandy!" he said. "It so happens that, in addition to having diabetes and being badly overweight, Mrs. Galway happens to have a nasty temper."

"Of course I don't blame her for being upset," Rita agreed, "after making all her plans to come in."

"She went to a lot of trouble," the old doctor observed. "Even phoned long distance to her married daughter to come down and look after her father while she's here. Now she's out there on a visitor's bench with nowhere to go."

Rita shook her head. "When you were here earlier, you said it was a simple problem."

"At that time I was sure I could catch her at home before she left," he said. "But it didn't turn out that way."

Rita consulted her files and sighed. "Well, we can't let her sit out in that lobby for two days," she said.

Dr. Arbo glanced warily toward the door.

"That's what she seems to think is going to happen. She stormed at me just now. I don't dare go back until we can think of some sort of story to tell her."

Rita glanced up at him. "Do you think she'd take a semi-private?"

"I'm sure she would," he said.

"There are three beds in this room," Rita said. "But it's all I can offer without using one of the emergency rooms."

"As long as I can find a corner to get her out of the lobby," the old man said. "As it is, I don't dare walk through there. She tackles me every time."

Rita laughed. "I'll call upstairs. It's 280, and she can be transferred to 227 on Saturday if she still wants a private room."

"Thank you!" Dr. Arbo looked relieved. "I don't know why you stick with this job and its headaches. Why don't you go back to regular nursing?"

"I think I'm more useful here," Rita said. "And I like it, in spite of the drawbacks."

Dr. Arbo took a few steps toward the door and then turned. "I heard about last night. That was a terrible accident. Strange that you and Paul should pass by just after it happened."

"I can't bear to think about it," Rita said. "It almost makes me afraid to drive."

He bowed his head gravely. "And those people in the second car were sitting on seat belts they hadn't bothered to use. It might have saved their lives if they'd had them on."

"And the ambulance was so slow in coming," Rita said. "Paul's very upset about it."

"I know," Dr. Arbo agreed. "I saw Fowler in the lobby a little while ago. I hear Dr. Francis had him on the carpet. He richly deserves it. He's one of the most uncooperative people we have in the building."

"Dr. Francis is bringing it up at the board meeting tonight," she said.

The thin man smiled grimly. "Should be some board meeting, with all the topics they'll be chewing on." And then: "I'd better get back and give Mrs. Galway the good news before she comes after me." With a grin, the old doctor hurried out.

Rita made a call arranging for Mrs. Galway to have the empty bed in 280 and then left on her rounds to pick up the floor reports. The head day nurse on the third floor was another veteran of many years at the hospital, a sour, efficient woman named Augusta Adair. The staff humorously referred to her behind her back as A.A. She was married, with grown children, and worked chiefly because she liked it.

Now Augusta Adair's black eyes snapped as she turned the reports over to Rita. She said: "You've loaded us up here! Why don't you send some of them to the second?"

"The second is just as heavy," Rita assured her.

"But we get the really complicated cases," Augusta Adair said sourly. "We're heavy with post-operatives, and the latest is that Mrs. Thomas, the leukemia case. She's in bad shape, and Dr. Solomon has set up a special routine with that new drug! I don't know how you people expect us to keep up with it. I'm skimped on staff and given all the hard patients."

It was an old story, one that Rita heard from the sour woman regularly. And yet she had to admit there was a good deal of truth in it. Although the cases were divided fairly between the floors and the second was as crowded as the third, there was a difference in the types of cases. The ones on third were more in need of frequent attention.

Rita said: "Perhaps Mrs. Thomas should have a private nurse. Have you talked to Dr. Solomon and her husband?"

Augusta Adair shrugged. "The husband had to leave for Portsmouth a little while ago. I'm going to speak to Dr. Solomon as soon as I can locate him. In the meantime, she's taking most of one nurse's time."

"And there is the problem of getting a private duty nurse," Rita said.

"We couldn't get one yesterday," the head nurse agreed in her gloomy way. "Only chance would be if one came off duty."

"You know, she must be very lonely," Rita reflected. "It would help her if she could have company. I think she'd really be better in a semi-private if you could find a congenial person."

August Adair gave her a grim look. "That mightn't be easy."

"I mean someone not too ill or talkative. Perhaps an older woman in for routine medical treatment who would enjoy taking an interest in her."

The sullen head nurse glared. "You're talking about a simple case. You'll only find them on the second floor."

Rita smiled. "You might be right at that." And she walked off to the elevator leaving the dour Augusta Adair watching after her with astonishment. The fact was that her chance remark had given Rita an idea.

By a remarkable coincidence, the first person she met when she reached the main lobby was Dr. Solomon. The cautious gray haired man was waiting to take the elevator in which she came down. She held him back by saying: "May I have a minute, Doctor?"

He nodded and stood with his head slightly to one side as he waited to hear what she had to say, his long face solemn as usual. "What is it, Miss Lewis?"

She quickly told him about Grace Thomas and the conclusions she'd reached. "I'd say she'd be better in a semi-private if she were with the right person, Doctor," she concluded.

Dr. Solomon nodded his agreement. "That's quite true, Miss Lewis. But as you point out, it would be necessary to find the proper person."

"Dr. Arbo has just brought in a patient I think might be suitable," Rita went on quickly. "A Mrs. Galway, who is in for diabetic treatment. She will be a walking patient, and she's well along in years. I'd judge she's a sensible person, if a little short-tempered."

The veteran doctor showed interest. "That might be a possibility, Miss Lewis. I'll talk it over with Dr. Arbo before I leave the hospital."

Rita returned to the office feeling a little lighter of heart. She might not have accomplished a thing, but at least she'd put forward her idea. If the two doctors agreed and both the patients showed interest, it might work out well all around. Now that she'd planted the seed, she'd have to wait to see if it developed. She was sure Grace Thomas would be better with company in that lonely room.

By working very hard, she managed to get the records looked after by three. She drove straight home and changed into her bathing suit, since it was another lovely, warm afternoon. Today the beach was more crowded, and she spent a little time talking with some of the neighbors she knew.

Helen Ferguson was there with the girls, and when Rita came by, she said: "Why don't you come over and visit with us tonight?"

Rita smiled down at her friend, who presented a matronly picture, her plump figure revealed by a skirted polka-dot bathing suit in blue and white. The two curly-headed blonde girls were scrapping over a pail of sand at her feet.

She said: "I would; only Paul promised to come by the cottage after the hospital meeting."

"That could be late," Helen reminded her. "Why don't you have him meet you at our place?"

"I might do that," Rita agreed. Taking a

glance at the lake, she said: "I'll take a swim and then rest for an hour or so on the beach."

"Find yourself a place a long way from us," Helen advised her. And then, with an annoyed little scream, she told the youngsters: "Will you two be quiet!"

Rita laughed and temporarily stopped their private battle by tousling the curly heads before she moved on to a deserted corner of the beach. She had her swim, then stretched out to rest.

She went over to the Fergusons about nine o'clock when she was sure the children had been put to bed. She knew if she came earlier, Helen would have to scold them to get them to go. When she arrived, Helen and Bill were sitting on their verandah. Helen had changed to a brown rayon dress, and Bill was sprawled out in their hammock, looking comfortable in a plaid shirt and dark slacks.

He smiled at Rita as she came onto the verandah. "Forgive me for being lazy," he said in his pleasant way. "This is the best spot I've hit today."

"Stay where you are," Rita said and, sitting on the verandah rail, surveyed him with an amused glance. "How's the back?"

"Great!" Bill said too enthusiastically.

"Hasn't bothered me any today. You can't beat your yellow pills."

"They're all gone," Rita said.

"And he wasn't so jolly about his back when he came home this afternoon." Helen spoke up, standing by the hammock with a worried air. "In fact, he took the last of those tablets you gave me yesterday."

Bill rolled his eyes good-naturedly. "You see what happens when you marry a woman who likes to worry? She finds trouble whether it exists or not."

"Maybe she'd relax if you'd see a doctor," Rita suggested.

Bill groaned and sat up in the hammock facing her. "Now I ask you. Do I look sick enough to go running to some doctor's office?"

She looked at his tanned, healthy young face. "You look all right," she admitted with a laugh.

Bill turned to his wife. "There! Now you've gotten an unprejudiced opinion."

Helen appeared unimpressed. "She doesn't have to listen to your complaints!"

"Wife, go get us some refreshment," he ordered with mock sternness. "On a night such as this, we need something to quench our thirst."

When Helen went inside, he stood up,

moved to the verandah post opposite Rita and leaned against it. "I guess that was some accident last night," he observed with a glance at the land fog that had come into the air with the growing darkness.

"It was a bad one," Rita admitted.

"I'll never forget that one I was in," Bill said, his intelligent face darkening. "I was unconscious off and on, but enough of it still comes back to me."

"You've never told us much about it."

"I'd rather not talk about it."

Rita could understand this, but she still pursued the subject. "I mean it would help if Paul knew exactly the type of back injuries you received," she said. "Then he'd understand more about your condition now."

"The accident had nothing to do with this trouble," Bill said emphatically.

"How can you be sure?"

This caught him without an argument. He glanced out at the lawn again, a touch of sullenness showing in his face. "I know you mean well, Rita. But I wish you'd not talk about it."

"But you should have your medical records after being in a serious accident like that," she said. "I'm only thinking of your own good. If you ever do need them, it could take a long time to get them."

"I know where they are," Bill said. "I'll send for them one of these days." But his voice carried no conviction, and he still avoided Rita's eyes.

She stared at him in the growing darkness. "We've heard so little about what you did in California, Bill. Paul was asking me the other day. You never seem to want to talk about it. I think it must be a fascinating country out there. I'd like to hear about your life before you came here."

Bill turned to her slowly. "My life began when I met Helen," he told her in a quiet voice. "There's nothing out there I want to remember."

So that was it. At least she'd gotten a straight reply from him. He didn't talk about his years on the West Coast because the memory of them was painful for some reason.

Helen returned with a tray of lemonade and cookies and so stopped Rita's speculations. But as they sat and chatted of the ordinary events of the day, her mind returned to the question of Bill's past. And she had a conviction there was something he wanted to conceal, something he felt he must conceal.

Bill broke into her thoughts by saying: "I hope Paul doesn't run into trouble at the board meeting tonight. There's a lot of talk going around town about Fowler being late with that ambulance last night."

So it had spread far enough for Bill to hear. She said: "I know. I think he'll be careful not to get himself too deeply involved in any controversy."

"Morton Gordon and his crowd are after Glen Parent's scalp, anyway," Bill went on. "They've never forgiven him for getting the mayoralty away from them."

"I know there's bad feeling," Rita said, sipping her lemonade.

Helen spoke from where she was sitting. "And Bill's heard rumors about some other people with political ambitions."

"That's right," Bill said with a touch of irony in his tone. "A good friend of yours is beginning to feel the urge for public service."

"Oh, yes?" she said, knowing Bill would go on.

"I overheard this at the office the other day," Bill continued. "Morton Gordon, Jr., and old Stanley Irwin were talking. I couldn't help hearing most of it. The main point was they thought Cliff Thomson might make a good candidate next election."

"Cliff Thomson!" Rita said in an incredulous tone.

"It struck me the same way!" Helen said disgustedly.

"They were serious enough," Bill assured them. "Old Irwin wants to push Cliff, now that he's one of the family. And he also thinks a new face would have a better chance of beating Glen Parent at the polls. Cliff is a sort of in-between in the town. He only got that big house in Greencrest lately. Before that he spent a lot of time with the ordinary crowd. They figure he knows enough people from both groups to win."

"But anyone who really knew Cliff well wouldn't think of him as the calibre of person to oppose Glen Parent for mayor," Rita protested.

Bill gave her an amused look. "But how many really do know him well? And you'll have to admit he puts on a big front."

She knew this was true. But she still couldn't picture the arrogant young Cliff as a serious contender for civic honors. She said: "It was probably just a lot of talk."

"That's what I say," her friend Helen agreed. "Old man Irwin just likes to hear himself sound off."

"Could be," Bill was willing to admit. "But it strikes me there's an awful lot of friction between Glen Parent and his councilmen and the business crowd headed by

Morton Gordon, Jr. and the wealthy Greencrest gang."

"I suppose they'll be using the hospital issues as a test of their strength," Rita said.

"Just what I'm thinking," Bill told her. "You can be sure Morton Gordon, Jr. will oppose anything the mayor suggests. I hope for Paul's sake he can keep from getting caught between the two groups."

"I hope so," Rita said with a sigh. But she realized this was what she'd been afraid of all along.

Chapter Six

The night wore on, and their talk drifted to other things. Twice Rita glanced at her wristwatch and noted that it was getting very late.

Helen asked: "Would you like some coffee, dear?"

Rita rose with a start. "No, thanks! And I really must go home. It looks as if Paul isn't going to make it."

Bill was on his feet now. "Probably that meeting is still going on."

Rita stared at him with incredulous eyes. "Do you actually think that?"

"Sure."

She sighed. "Well, I'm glad I didn't decide to spend the evening waiting by myself." She thanked them both hurriedly, got into her car and drove back to the cottage.

After she had turned on the lights, she really began to worry. What could have happened that Paul hadn't shown up? And he hadn't even phoned to let her know.

She suddenly realized that in her agitated

frame of mind she had been pacing back and forth in her living room without even being aware of it. Then the phone rang, and she found herself racing to answer it.

It was Paul, who said: "I guessed you'd probably left Fergusons'. I've just left the meeting."

"I've been so worried!" she exclaimed. "How did it go?"

He gave a weary chuckle. "If you really want to know, put the coffee on. I'm on my way over."

She'd just gotten the coffee nicely percolating and made a few hastily prepared cheese sandwiches when his car came into the driveway. She switched on the outside light and pushed open the screen door for him.

His face showed tired lines as he stepped into the bright light of the living room. He paused to take her in his arms and kiss her briefly; then, with an arm still around her, he walked with her to the kitchen.

He dropped into a chair by the arborite table. "I'm bushed!" he said in a completely exhausted tone.

She poured him a cup of coffee and one for herself. "Did you just now finish?"

He nodded as she pushed the plate of sandwiches toward him and sat at the table so they were facing each other. "It was a jam session," he said. "But Glen Parent won by a hair."

Rita smiled. "I hope that's good news."

"I'd say so." He took a sandwich.

"What about you and the ambulance thing?"

He shook his head. "Francis got that out of the way early. He said Fowler had behaved in an insubordinate manner when he questioned him and threatened to quit his job. I guess this has been going on for some time. He has a brother in the West who wants him to come out there. So Francis told him to go."

"He fired him?"

Paul nodded. "That's right. Morton Gordon, Jr. contended it was the fault of the man and not the system. I got up and said I thought it was wrong to depend on a maintenance man to double as driver unless priority was given to his work with the ambulance."

Rita said: "What was the reaction to that?"

"Mixed. Morton Gordon, Jr. said that any lazy maintenance man could use his ambulance duties as an excuse to shirk repair work. Glen Parent thought my idea was good. But he also said it was important to have the right man for the job."

"Did they settle on anything?"

Paul shrugged. "It ended about as I expected. They're going to put the ruling I suggested into effect. But the ambulance will still be operated by a maintenance man." He gave her a weary grin. "Then the curtain went up on the big show."

"You mean Dr. Francis officially resigned?"

"Right. Of course that brought expressions of alarm and regret, as the newspapers will say tomorrow, though most of those on the board knew it before they came. Morton Gordon, Jr. rumbled something about a replacement, and right away Dr. Francis came up with this Dr. Grant's name."

She said: "Glen Parent's cousin?"

He nodded. "Well, that got off the ground with a bang. Old man Irwin began to question his qualifications, Morton Gordon, Jr. thought a wide search should be made for candidates for the job first, and one of the Barrys suggested Dr. Francis be given an increase in salary if he'd stay."

"So?"

"So no one was happy. Dr. Francis refused to stay and said they had to find a replacement soon or he'd leave in any case. He was strongly in favor of Dr. Grant and stressed they would find difficulty getting anyone else as good. Glen Parent said nothing for or against his cousin. But when the vote was taken, the councilman and his crowd won by two votes."

"I can imagine Morton Gordon, Jr.'s happy reaction," Rita said dryly.

Paul drained his cup of coffee and pushed it across to her to be refilled. He said: "There was plenty of yelling and loud talk. I kept out of it altogether. For once I took your advice."

Rita smiled as she poured his coffee. "Live to fight another day," she said.

He looked at her with questioning eyes. "And what do you suppose most of the up-roar was about?"

"Them deciding on the mayor's cousin for the job?"

He shook his head. "No, although of course we both knew that was the main reason. But the reason they gave was quite different. Morton Gordon, Jr. raised Cain because they chose a woman to be the new superintendent."

It was Rita's turn to show shock. "A woman?"

Paul laughed. "I thought that would get you. It wasn't one of Glen Parent's male cousins who became a doctor. It was one of the female Grants, Dr. Mary Grant."

"I can't believe it," Rita said.

"You should have heard them." Paul continued to chuckle at the memory of it. "They claimed a woman couldn't do the job, that she'd have the hospital in a mess in a couple of months."

"Then you really think she's capable?" Rita asked.

Paul gave a surprised glance. "Don't tell me you doubt your own sex?"

"Well, no." She hesitated. "But it is a bit unusual. I haven't heard of many women superintendents."

"There have been quite a few," Paul maintained, "considering the fact there are not a lot of women doctors. And Mary Grant has been extremely successful with a small hospital in Maine."

Rita smiled. "You seem very satisfied with the appointment."

"I am," he admitted. "I happen to know Mary. She did some work at the clinic when I was there. We got to be pretty good friends."

"Well!" Rita said, looking at him with knowing eyes.

Paul showed some slight embarrassment. "Now don't go getting any wrong ideas because I said we were friends," he said. "We were just that — casual friends. We went to a couple of parties together and to a movie once or twice. Then she left, and I haven't heard of her since."

Rita said: "You sound pretty enthusiastic about her for such a casual friend."

He looked at her. "Don't you believe me?"

She smiled. "I certainly want to." And then: "What sort of person is she?"

"Got a terrific mind," he said. "I mean the scientific type you don't look for in a female. And she has a way of handling situations and people."

"I'm not interested in her as a diplomat, or in her mind either," she said with a wry smile. "I want to know if she's pretty."

Again Paul looked embarrassed, and she was almost sure he blushed. "She's not ugly," he said. "She has plenty of charm. But she's years older than you. Must be thirty-six or seven."

"Close to your age," she reminded him quietly.

"That's right," he admitted.

"I can't remember her," Rita said, "but I'll be interested in her."

"Well, it looks like you will," Paul told her.

"When is she coming?"

"Within two weeks," Paul said. "Dr. Francis is leaving in a month."

"Well, that will mean some changes," Rita

said. "I can't say I envy her the job, with the Gordon crowd against her."

Paul put down his empty cup. "She'll need all the support she can get."

Rita gave him a teasing smile. "Well, at least she can count on one friend. She'll be delighted to see you."

He laughed. "Don't joke about it! I may be the only one on her side. I doubt if Dr. Solomon or even Dr. Arbo will be overjoyed at having a woman chief." He got up. "I'll go home and let you get some rest."

Of course the word spread through the hospital like wildfire. For some it was a joke, while for the more serious-minded it was a reason to shake heads. The truth was that most of the staff were willing to wait and accept or reject Dr. Mary Grant on her capabilities; it was the extremists who were making all the comments.

Laura Graham was not one of these. She told Rita: "I don't see why this Grant girl can't do as well as Francis. And I hear she's a specialist in ear, nose and throat. We need somebody in that field here."

Rita stared across the desk at the superintendent of nurses. "I'm sure she has the qualifications," she said. "I just hope she'll be given the chance to prove them."

The older nurse sighed. "I know what you

mean. People aren't noted for their fairness. And she'll be caught between Gordon and the others."

"The whole idea will be difficult to sell the public," Rita said. "So any criticisms that are brought up will be given more attention than they probably would get under other circumstances."

Dr. Jonas Arbo walked briskly into the office, a smile on his face. "Well, a good morning to you, ladies," he said. "I presume you have heard the good news. Maybe there'll be a chance for this widower after all."

Laura Graham gave him a scornful glance. "You surely don't think a young woman like Dr. Mary Grant would take any notice of a wizened old codger like you?"

The spare, bald man turned a doleful face to Rita. "Now I ask you, would you call that fair?"

Rita stifled a laugh. "She's probably jealous," she said with a side glance in Laura Graham's direction.

The white-haired nurse bridled. "Jealous! If that were the case, I'd need my head examined."

"An excellent suggestion." Dr. Arbo bowed slightly. "I shall be most happy to accommodate you, miss. My office hours are two to four on alternate afternoons."

The veteran nurse shook her head. "A clear case of second childhood," she told Rita, and went back to her work.

Dr. Jonas winked at Rita. "In order to disprove your colleague's unfair comment, I wish to say I'm here on a business matter."

Rita smiled. "Fine."

"Also, may I congratulate you on an excellent idea?" he continued. "Both ladies are in agreement with it, and I'd like to have you transfer Mrs. Galway to Mrs. Thomas' room on the third floor."

"I'll look after it," Rita promised. "I'll have an extra bed put in 318. It really is a semi-private room." She paused to raise questioning eyes to the old doctor's face. "You're sure they'll get along?"

He beamed at her. "Indeed I am. Mrs. Galway, who was not happy on the second floor, paid a preliminary visit to Mrs. Thomas before making a decision. And of course she fell in love with the charming little lady. Say what you will about Mrs. Galway's temper, she has a kind heart and a glib line of conversation. It's my guess she'll do that poor girl as much good as Dr. Solomon's wonder drug."

"I thought she must be lonely," Rita agreed.

"It's all settled," Dr. Arbo said. "You may

go ahead with the transfer." He turned to Laura Graham. "And you, Miss Graham, may regret your tartness of tongue should I emerge as the husband of our new superintendent." With a quick wink in Rita's direction, he made a hasty exit before Laura Graham could reply.

Rita didn't see Paul Reid all morning, but they did meet in the cafeteria at noon hour and shared a table. Paul looked somewhat tired after his busy evening.

He smiled at her across the table. "What have you heard on the gossip line this morning? What seems to be the general opinion?"

She laughed. "Dr. Arbo hopes she might be interested in matrimony."

"I've talked with Arbo," Paul said. "He's all for her."

"I had an idea he was," Rita agreed. "Otherwise he wouldn't have been in such a jolly mood."

"We could do with more like him in the hospital," the young doctor said with a slight frown. "I was surprised at Dr. Solomon. I think he's lining up with Morton Gordon, Jr. and his crowd."

"Well, that wouldn't be so surprising," Rita pointed out. "Don't forget he's the doctor for most of the wealthy people in town."

"He also happens to be an excellent one," Paul said. "I expected him to show more fairness in this matter. He seems prejudiced against working under the Grant girl not only because she's a female but because she's Glen Parent's cousin."

"And a former one of the have-nots in Riverdale," Rita suggested.

"That seems to hurt some," he admitted.

"I didn't have a chance to mention it last night," she said. "But Bill told me the Irwins are going to push Cliff Thomson politically."

Paul showed the astonishment she expected. "Now I've heard everything," he said. "How can they be so optimistic?"

"I don't know," she said. "Bill seemed to think that, with the Irwin money and Gordon support as well, he might do all right."

"Stranger things have happened," Paul agreed grimly. And changing the subject: "I'm sorry I didn't get to the Fergusons' last night. I missed seeing Bill. How was he?"

"It's hard to say," Rita worried. "He pretended he was all right. I asked him about his accident and why he didn't send to California for his medical history, and he became quite upset."

"Upset?"

Rita nodded. "I'd say he acted very

strangely, as though he had something he didn't want anyone to find out; something that happened out there he's ashamed of."

Paul showed some doubt. "I can't believe that. He's probably too busy to want to bother sending letters and getting the information. It could take some time and trouble."

"But if he's having a recurrence of the trouble, he should have his charts available," she said.

"Agreed. But you know how stubborn he is." He sat back in his chair and glanced around the crowded room. "I'll bet half the talk going on here is about last night's meeting."

She smiled. "It could easily be."

He looked at her again. "By the way, I need a room for an emergency this afternoon."

"An honest-to-goodness emergency?" she asked. "Or are you another one looking for special favors?"

"Not guilty," he said. "I'll come around officially after we go upstairs. It's the older Mr. Mason. I checked his X-rays this morning. He has a serious partial bladder obstruction. I'm arranging for emergency surgery in the morning. I want him in this afternoon."

"Does it look bad?" she said.

"I don't like it," Paul admitted with a sigh. "That's why I want to get at it without delay."

"It's a fairly serious operation," Rita said. "How's his general health?"

"Good for his age," Paul said. "That's why I don't want to let this go. A cystotomy could bring him back to full health. At this point I wouldn't call it a serious risk."

"Unless the obstruction turned out to be a malignancy."

"There is that chance," he agreed. "But the majority of them don't turn out to be. I'm hoping we'll be lucky this time."

"I hope so, too," Rita said. "Mr. Mason is a fine old man. I suppose you'll need the room for at least two weeks."

He nodded. "That should be plenty of time if there are no complications."

"I'll try to get you something on the second floor," Rita said. "Augusta Adair is complaining about being overworked upstairs." And she got up.

Paul rose with her. "Too bad Augusta is such a good nurse. Otherwise I'd put in a complaint against her. She's a gloom chaser."

Rita went back to her desk and worked until it was time to pick up the reports from the floor supervisors again. When she reached the third floor, Augusta Adair met her in an ugly mood.

"So you've changed 318 to a semi-private," she said. "I suppose you'll want to make wards of all the rooms. Where do you think the nurses are coming from to look after these new patients?"

Rita smiled. "I don't think Mrs. Galway will add much to your worries."

Augusta Adair's black eyes snapped. "She's a diabetic with a special course of treatment."

"But I think she'll be company for Mrs. Thomas," Rita pointed out. "And that should make things easier on that score."

The head nurse sat down at her desk with a shrug. "Well, it's done. No one asks my advice."

"Don't you agree?"

"I suppose so," Augusta Adair said grudgingly. "The last time I was in there, they were twittering like a pair of lovebirds."

"I'm glad of that," Rita said. "Grace Thomas is such a bad case. It makes my heart ache to think about her. I'm sure you must feel the same way."

The sour head nurse stared at her stonily. "Miss Lewis, you talk like a newcomer to our profession. Frankly, I'm surprised. If I were to indulge in your sort of sentimental attitude I'd be sitting here weeping all day." She paused before continuing acidly, "Perhaps you've stayed too long in the front office. You've lost perspective."

"I don't think it's so much a matter of perspective," Rita said quietly, "as it is one of temperament. I'm sorry to have presumed, Mrs. Adair."

She managed to make her reply polite, but she walked away from the sour head nurse with a feeling of anger. She made her way to 318.

When she entered the room, both women were in bed and talking. They paused in their conversation at her entrance, and Grace Thomas smiled happily at her. Rita was pleased to see her in such good spirits.

"Rita," the fragile young wife said, "I was hoping you'd be around. I knew you came at this time." She nodded toward the other bed. "I want you to meet Mrs. Galway."

"I've heard a great deal about you, Mrs. Galway," Rita said with a smile, turning to the other bed.

Mrs. Galway was apparently in her late fifties, with a florid, pleasant face. She returned Rita's smile. "I imagine Dr. Arbo told you the state I was in. He calls me his old crank."

"He says many nicer things about you when you're not around," Rita said.

"Well, that's encouraging," the stout woman said. "And I do appreciate your arranging for me to come up here, though the nurse in charge of this floor is a battle-axe."

"She's not as bad as she pretends," Rita said. "And she is competent."

"So I've been told," Mrs. Galway said. "In any case, it doesn't matter. I can hold my own. I'm considered a battle-axe myself."

"She's a darling!" Grace Thomas told Rita. "And I do feel so much better." Rita was impressed by the girl's animation, and she did have a hint of color in her pale cheeks.

"How are the treatments?" Rita asked.

"They haven't bothered me any so far," Grace said. "And I do feel better. I've had a phone call from Mother. Jack will be back tomorrow for a visit, and he's going to pick her up on the way."

Rita could see the happy anticipation in the sick girl's eyes and felt a wave of sympathy for her.

She smiled. "I'll have to be on my way now. I'll stop by again whenever I'm up here."

"Please do," Grace said. And Mrs. Galway added her own thanks.

Rita went downstairs, feeling she had at least accomplished some good.

Soon after she returned to her desk, Dr. Solomon presented himself before her. The veteran practitioner seemed in a depressed mood. He nodded brusquely and said: "I've come about Mrs. Barry."

"Oh, yes," Rita said, referring to her list. "We have her booked for Monday."

"So Dr. Francis informs me," the gray-haired man said. He cleared his throat. "Dr. Francis informed me about Morton Gordon, Jr.'s behavior the other day and your decision following it."

"I see," Rita said, looking at him with questioning eyes.

He again cleared his throat. "I agree with Dr. Francis the whole affair has been most unfortunate."

"Well, it seems to be cleared up now," Rita said.

"I'm afraid it isn't," Dr. Solomon said. "I must ask you for a room for my patient at once."

Rita showed surprise. "Is this an order from Dr. Francis?"

"It is," Dr. Solomon said with a show of impatience. "Please see that a room is prepared at once. My patient is on the way here now in the ambulance." And he turned abruptly and hurried out.

She was somewhat shocked by his

manner. She had never known Dr. Solomon to be so curt and agitated. He was normally very much the old school doctor, quiet and gentlemanly.

With a sigh she checked off one of her two remaining emergency rooms and put a call through to the second floor to confirm Mrs. Barry's reservation. She had just put down the phone when Dr. Francis' short, wiry figure appeared in the doorway.

The superintendent gave a cautious glance to ascertain that Laura Graham was not in the room and then came over to Rita with a troubled look on his face.

"I'm glad to find you alone," he said. "I suppose Dr. Solomon has been by to see you?"

"Yes," she said. "I've given one of the emergency rooms to Mrs. Barry."

Dr. Francis rubbed the palms of his hands together nervously. "Yes. That is fine." He glanced toward the door warily and then leaned forward to say: "This is in strict confidence. But there is a reason for the change of plans. Dr. Solomon has just returned from Mrs. Barry's residence. She took an overdose of sleeping tablets this morning in an attempt to end her life!"

Chapter Seven

Rita entered the name of Mrs. Roger Barry on her records and in brackets after it (Ellen, May). It was as Ellen May Gordon she had known her during her school days in Riverdale. Of course Ellen May had been several years older and in an advanced grade. But as one of the Gordons and destined to inherit a great deal of money one day, she had been the center of envious eyes.

Her schoolmates often speculated on the wonderful life she must lead and the exciting future that surely was ahead for her. And Ellen May, a laughing, carefree girl with a neat figure and pretty face, seemed to take it all for granted. Rita had known her in a brief school friendship when the older girl had come to her rescue during a snowball battle between some of the younger boys and girls. All Rita's pigtailed cohorts had deserted her, and she was forlornly trying to hold her own against a barrage of snowballs from the boys' side when Ellen May, who happened to be passing, had thrown aside her books and joined in the fray on Rita's side.

Whether it was the sight of an older Gordon taking arms against them or the fact Ellen May threw a very good snowball was something Rita had never been able to decide, but within a few minutes the boys had trailed off, shouting back suitable derisive epithets.

Ellen May, dark, with laughing eyes, and extravagantly pretty in a pale blue snow hood and white jacket of some imitation fur, had turned to Rita and said: "What ever made you take on all those boys by yourself?"

Rita, a full six inches shorter and still spindly, had bravely managed a smile and said: "It didn't start out that way."

Ellen May retrieved her books from the snow, and they both began to walk toward their homes. "I see," the older girl said. "You were the victim of deserters."

"I don't know where they went so fast," Rita said with a shake of her head.

With a wisdom beyond her years, Ellen May had nodded and told her: "You have to be prepared for that. You often find yourself alone when the going gets difficult."

Now, staring at the entry she'd made on

her records and knowing the significant story behind it, Rita wondered how difficult the going had been for poor Ellen May and how alone she must have felt to bring her to this point of despair. She made up her mind to see this friend of her school days if a proper opportunity presented itself.

Rita and Laura Graham were in the lobby together on Saturday morning when a tall, distinguished-looking man with silver-white hair and a bloated, purplish face strode in through the front entrance and made his way to the elevators, where he pressed the button and waited impatiently.

The veteran nurse touched Rita's arm and murmured: "That's Roger Barry, Ellen May's husband."

Rita gave him another quick glance as he vanished into the elevator. Then she turned to Laura and said: "But he's so old! He must be thirty years older than she is."

Laura Graham nodded knowingly. "And don't tell me that isn't one of the main reasons she's up there in that condition."

Rita had seen little of Paul since the night of the meeting. They'd talked briefly at the hospital and planned to attend the country club dance on Saturday night as usual. In the meantime they had both been occupied with their work.

Paul had brought in his patient with the bladder obstruction and operated on him. Mr. Mason's condition was excellent and there had been no trace of a malignancy.

Dr. Solomon had acted rather shy since his nervous outburst on the day he'd had to face the emergency with Mrs. Roger Barry. He had been in to see Rita several times, but on each occasion he had made their exchange as brief as possible and hurried away.

On Saturday morning he came in again. But this time he seemed a little less uneasy. Rita cleared up a minor problem for him and then took the liberty of mentioning Grace Thomas.

"How is Mrs. Thomas responding?" she asked.

The solemn-faced doctor smiled sadly. "She is doing much better with your therapy than with mine," he said. "Your Mrs. Galway has done her a great deal of good, and she watches over her like a mother hen."

Rita was pleased to hear this. "I'm glad," she said. "It was a risk."

Dr. Solomon adjusted his glasses. "Whenever one tries to accomplish anything, there is always a risk. I had hopes Mrs. Thomas would show a better response to this new drug."

"You can't notice any improvement?"

"Perhaps it is too soon," the old man said heavily. "But she has been ill a long time, you know. Only her husband still hopes for a miracle."

"It's a hard thing to face," Rita said. "And she's so young and attractive."

"I agree." He sighed. "Well, we keep on trying, eh?" And with that he left the office.

Shortly before noon, Rita saw Captain Jack Thomas in the main lobby with a thin, harried-looking woman who walked with a cane. She was having difficulty managing the short distance between the front door and the elevators. Rita didn't want to intrude at this difficult moment and decided she'd wait and probably see the young officer later.

There was no sign of him in the cafeteria, but she did meet Winnie, the day telephone operator. Winnie was full of gossip as usual.

The thin woman leaned across the table confidentially and told Rita: "Did you know Roger Barry is having one of those big mental specialists come down from Boston to see his wife?"

"No," Rita said. "Do they think she's mentally ill?"

The telephone operator shrugged. "Well, from what I heard, they can't find anything else wrong with her, so they've decided it has to be nerves." Winnie made a face. "I guess around here we'd call it plain crazy."

Rita gave her a reproving smile. "I doubt if she's as bad as all that."

Winnie buttered a piece of bread and said complacently: "All I know is Dr. Solomon told this man there was nothing more he could do for her. The specialist said he'd come down here the first of the week."

"We'll know more about it then," Rita said, glancing around the crowded cafeteria to see if she could locate Paul. But there was no sign of the young surgeon.

Winnie leaned forward again with a conspiratorial smile. "Oh, yes. I heard the woman who's going to be our new super on the phone. That Grant girl!"

Rita's interest was caught again. "Did you?"

Winnie nodded. "Yes. She's called a couple of times. Got a nice soft voice and seems pleasant enough, though I must say I can't see her running a place like this."

"She may surprise you," Rita said with a smile.

"She'll have to," Winnie said, hunching importantly in her chair. "I've worked under three supers in this hospital, and I can't see a woman doing the job. I say she'd never gotten it if she hadn't been the mayor's cousin!"

Rita was surprised at the telephone operator's attitude. Apparently the rift between the opposing factions was beginning to show itself all down the line. She would have expected Winnie to be on the side of the have-nots, since she was one herself. But on the other hand, she might have guessed the gossipy woman would line herself up with the Riverdale aristocracy.

After lunch she made her usual rounds to pick up the daily reports. On Saturday she did this somewhat earlier. When she reached the third floor, she found another woman in Augusta Adair's place. The sour nurse took Saturday off, according to her replacement, and worked on Sundays instead.

Rita wondered if she should go down to see Grace Thomas. She wouldn't have a chance again until Monday. But the sick girl did have visitors, and with Mrs. Galway in the room, it would be rather crowded. She decided she'd better wait for another time and made her way to the elevators.

She'd just pressed the button when a familiar figure in a kimono made an appearance in the doorway of the small alcove reserved for visitors. It was Mrs. Galway.

The stout woman advanced on Rita with a

broad smile. "I thought it was you," she said.

Rita returned the smile. "What are you doing away out here?"

Mrs. Galway winked at her. "I brought Mrs. Thomas' mother up to the visitors' room to sit with me awhile. Only right to give the young people a little privacy. They don't see much of each other these days."

Rita was touched by the thought of the diabetes patient. She said: "I'm sure they appreciate what you've done. How are you feeling?"

Mrs. Galway's face clouded. "I'm afraid I'm a lot better."

Rita laughed. "That's a new kind of complaint! I must tell Dr. Arbo."

Mrs. Galway's broad, motherly face took on an embarrassed look. "I don't mean it the way I sound." She sighed. "I just hate to go and leave her alone."

"Everyone thinks you've helped her wonderfully," Rita said.

Mrs. Galway's eyes met hers in forlorn appeal. "She's going to die, isn't she?"

Rita was caught off guard. "We hope she'll be better," she hedged.

The older woman shook her head. "I know. And I've watched that Dr. Solomon's face when he comes in the room and checks on her. I've been around too long. No one has to tell me."

"The main thing is to keep her as comfortable as possible," Rita said. "And you've helped in that."

"I don't forget it was your idea," Mrs. Galway said. "And neither does she. Both she and her husband think you're wonderful." She shook her head. "But I say it's wrong for an old crank like me to get better and for that poor thing to stay here and die."

"Don't worry about it," Rita said quietly. "And you can come back and see her."

"It won't be the same," Mrs. Galway grumbled. "And don't tell Arbo I feel better. I may be able to fool him awhile longer."

Rita laughed. "You just pretend to be worse, and maybe you'll manage to stay on for the rest of the summer."

"I doubt it," Mrs. Galway said. "He's sharp." And then: "Well, I must go back and sit with her mother. She's terribly crippled with arthritis. And of course she's upset, poor creature!" The buxom woman in the kimono nodded and then hurried back into the alcove.

The rest of the day was uneventful, and Rita stopped at the supermarket on the way home to do her usual weekend shopping. When this was done, she went to a small bakery nearby and picked up some homemade bread and an orange cake Paul liked.

She was on her way back to the car when a serious-faced young man in a dark suit came up to her and said: "Hello, Rita!"

She glanced at him in surprise and saw that it was the mayor, Glen Parent. She smiled. "Hello, Glen! You looked so solemn I didn't recognize you."

He laughed. "And you're so pretty these days, I almost didn't know you." He reached for her parcels. "Let me take those, and I'll walk you as far as your car."

Rita studied him with amused eyes. "I'm not used to such gallantry!"

Glen took the parcels. "It's not gallantry. It's an excuse. I don't see much of you these days."

"Nor I you," she said. They strolled across the busy street in the direction of the supermarket parking lot where Rita had left her car.

The young man eyed the traffic with grim resignation. "Almost worth your life to get across there on a Saturday. Things have certainly changed in Riverdale."

"I think so," Rita said with a smile. "Look what a wonderful mayor we have."

"Your enthusiasm isn't shared by everyone in town," he said. "Or perhaps you already know that."

"Well, isn't opposition always a healthy thing?" she said.

Glen gave her a rueful smile. "It could be that mine is just a mite too healthy."

"I heard you did very well on the hospital issue," Rita said. "Of course that's one of the things that directly concerns me."

Glen nodded. "I hope I did right. I didn't vote myself, since Mary is my cousin. But they put her in."

"It will be interesting to work with a woman as superintendent," she said.

"Not everyone at the hospital thinks so." Glen frowned. "I've had some letters from one or two doctors already."

They had reached her car now, and she stopped and stared up at him with astonishment. "You mean they're complaining even before they know how she's going to make out?"

"That's it," he said. "At least I can count on Paul. That's one thing about your Dr. Reid," he said. "He's fair, whatever the cost."

Rita unlocked her car door and glanced back at him. "I think he knows Dr. Grant as well."

Glen nodded and stood ready to hand her the parcels as she slid behind the wheel of her car. "So I hear," he said. "They were friends when she was out in the Middle West."

Rita smiled as she took the packages from him. "So it all may work out very well."

Glen stood there with a dubious expression. "I'd like to think that," he said. "But I know Morton Gordon, Jr., and his crowd are going to start a lot of trouble just as soon as she gets here."

"I have confidence in you and Paul," she said. "Are you coming to the club dance tonight?"

"Maybe," he said. "Depends on how things shape up later in the day." He waved as she drove away.

Most of her housework had to be done on weekends. By the time she got home from the hospital on a regular working day, she was too tired to do much more than the light work. As soon as she'd put her groceries away, she changed to slacks and blouse and took out the mop and pail to give the floors their weekly cleaning.

With this and other tasks, the afternoon passed quickly. She was dusting off pictures and ornaments in the living room when she heard a car in the driveway. Glancing out, she saw that it was Helen Ferguson in the station wagon. She put aside her duster and went out on the verandah to meet her friend.

The buxom Helen was also in slacks and blouse, with a brown kerchief tied over her head to cover her curlers. She mounted the steps of the verandah with a small smile.

"Another scorcher of a day," she said.

Rita nodded. "I'm dead. I've been working ever since I got home." She flopped down on the wicker settee and waved to Helen to join her.

Her friend sat down. "I wondered why you didn't stop."

"I was in a hurry to get home," Rita said. "What are you going to wear to the club tonight?"

Helen looked suddenly forlorn. "I'm afraid we can't go."

"Oh, no!"

Her friend sighed. "Same old thing. He came home early with that back again."

Rita became indignant. "He's not being fair to you or himself," she said. "He's got to have medical attention. I'll have Paul stop by before we go to the club."

"He'll be angry!" Helen warned. But there was not the usual strong protest in her

118

manner, and Rita felt she would appreciate Paul coming by.

"Let him be," she said scornfully. "I'm angry because he's spoiled our evening. It isn't much fun for Paul and me to go to the club alone."

"I'm disappointed, too," Helen said, looking down at her hands. "I spent a lot of time on my hair this morning and had my white dress pressed and ready to wear."

"This nonsense about not wanting to see a doctor has to end," Rita said.

Helen gave her a worried glance. "You know, Rita," she said, "I'm beginning to think there's some special reason he doesn't want a doctor."

Rita had been thinking the same thing for some time. But it was the first time Helen had ever said anything to suggest she might have had the same thought. Rita leaned forward.

"What do you mean?" she asked.

Helen shook her head. "One of the things he's afraid of is that a doctor will want his old medical records. And he's always been so mysterious about his life in California."

"I know that," Rita agreed, sensing that her friend had more to say and anxious to hear what it might be.

"I've never pried," Helen went on, a wor-

119

ried look on her pleasant, round face. "We've been happy, and that's enough for me. But lately I've worried."

"Have you said anything to him?"

"No," Helen said. "But when I was house-cleaning last week, I decided to throw out one of his old suitcases. It was a battered old thing he's brought here with him from the West in his bachelor days. I decided to check through the pockets to make sure there was nothing left in it, and I found this." She took a printed slip from her pocket and handed it to her.

Rita took the slip and studied it. It was a driver's license for California dated ten years back. She said: "What about it?"

"See the name it's made out to." Helen pointed. "Wallace Fuller. It's a different name, but the initials are the same as Bill's — William Ferguson!" The eyes of the two women met, and Rita saw the pleading fear in Helen's.

She said: "You surely don't think —"

"I don't know!" Helen turned away with a small moan of anguish.

Rita stared down at the license again and considered.

"Bill has brushes, a letter case and other things from the old days," Helen went on, "all with his initials on them." She paused.

"And now I realize they may have stood for another name."

"You actually think Bill changed his name for some reason?"

"I'm beginning to," Helen admitted. She turned to Rita with fear on her round face. "And I don't know what it means. I'm afraid it might be something terrible."

"Of course not!" Rita replied too quickly. She couldn't bear to see Helen's distress. "You know the sort of person Bill is. So do we all. I'm sure there's a perfectly good explanation for this." She handed the paper back to Helen.

"Do you really think so?"

Rita nodded. "I do. And don't torment yourself with a lot of nonsense any more. When you find a proper time, ask Bill about the license. But I wouldn't bother him until he's feeling better."

Helen gave a small relieved sigh. "I feel better already after talking to you about it. I hope you don't mind?"

Rita smiled and patted her friend's hand. "I'm glad you did tell me. And we'll stop by and see Bill on the way to the dance."

Helen left, after thanking her again, and Rita thought she looked less worried.

Before she knew it, dinner had arrived. She ate lightly, as she often did on warm nights, and then took a quick cold shower. By the time Paul's car entered the driveway she had put on her chiffon evening dress and was just attaching the second of her favorite dangling gold earrings.

He let himself in the screen door and called out: "Anyone home?"

She came to join him with a smile. "My, you look handsome for a change," she said. She always admired him in his white dinner jacket and black tie.

Paul regarded her with appraising eyes. "I think you'll do as my lady of the evening. Yes, I'd say you'll do very well." And he reached out and took her hands.

Rita gave him a teasing smile. "At least until a certain lady doctor comes along."

"Let's put that subject right out of our minds," he said, and drew her to him for a kiss.

She looked at him with humorous despair. "Now you're all lipstick," she worried. She took his white handkerchief from his upper jacket and cleaned away the traces of crimson. "That's better," she said, giving it back to him.

"Where are the Fergusons?" he asked. "I thought we were all going in my car."

Rita shook her head. "They can't come tonight."

He frowned. "Not that back of his again?"

"Yes." She nodded. "I promised you'd come by and take a look at him. Helen said he'd be angry, but she seemed to want you to do it just the same."

"I will," he said. "I'm anxious to talk to him about that back."

Rita looked at him with worried eyes. "Don't say too much tonight. Give him something for the pain. But don't ask too many questions, especially not questions about his old medical record."

Paul showed surprise. "Why not?"

"I can't take the time to tell you now," she said. "But take my word for it: there's a good reason." And she led the way to the door.

Chapter Eight

"Well, here we are," Paul said with a sigh as they pulled up in front of the Ferguson place. "I have my bag locked in the trunk; I'll get it."

Rita waited until he'd gotten his bag, and then they both went up the steps to the verandah. Rita pressed the bell, and they waited a minute.

Helen came to the door with an apologetic air. "I'm so sorry to have kept you waiting," she said, pushing the screen door open. "I was in the back playroom with the children, watching television."

"We just got here," Paul said.

Helen gave them a forlorn smile. "The master of the house is upstairs in the bedroom," she said.

Paul nodded. "I'll go on up and see what's happening," he said, and made his way up the stairs.

Rita turned to Helen. "I like your dress. It's too bad you can't come with us."

The stout girl shrugged. "Maybe another weekend."

"We'll plan on that," Rita said with a smile.

Helen looked worried. After a careful glance upstairs, she moved closer to Rita and said in a low voice: "About what I mentioned to you this afternoon: I've been thinking it's silly! Probably that license belonged to some friend of Bill's, maybe even someone he loaned the bag to. It can't be important."

Rita knew Helen well enough to see she was badly frightened and trying hard to cover up. She felt the only thing to do was to play along with her and try and give her some peace of mind. She said: "I told you that when we were talking."

Helen nodded. "Just forget all about it. I'm going to."

"Of course," Rita said. But she knew that Helen wasn't going to forget, nor was she. It was a pathetic little game they were playing.

Helen looked toward the upstairs again. "I'm glad Paul's seeing him," she said. "Maybe now he'll be sensible."

"I'm sure Paul will find out what's wrong and see that he does something about it," Rita agreed. But again she was by no means as certain as she was trying to sound.

A few minutes later Paul came down, and Rita could tell at once by the slight shadow of concern on his handsome face that he was not satisfied with what he'd seen. She met him at the foot of the stairs and asked: "How did you make out?"

The young doctor glanced at her and then at Helen with a deep sigh. "He's got some sort of nerve trouble; that's my guess," he said. "I'd like to have him come by my office the first of the week. Then I can give him a proper examination."

"Do you think it's serious?" Helen asked.

Paul looked at the stout girl's worried face. "I think it's painful," he said, evading a direct answer. "I've left some tablets that will carry him over the weekend."

"That's good," Helen said, sounding relieved. "And I'll give him a good talking to. I'll make sure he does go to your office, Paul."

"Do that." Paul nodded.

They talked a few minutes longer and went back to the car. Helen waited on the verandah to wave them on their way. Rita thought she looked troubled and forlorn. She was beginning to have serious misgivings about the future of this nice little family. She waited until they were well along the road leading to the main highway before she questioned the young doctor about Bill.

"How was he?" she asked.

Paul kept his eyes on the road ahead, but his expression became grim. "I'd say he was suffering a great deal of pain." He paused. "Have you ever seen him in a bathing suit?"

Rita considered. "I must have. He and Helen often bring the children down to the beach."

"Have you or haven't you?" Paul queried in an almost irritable tone.

"I guess so," she faltered, surprised at his manner. "I can't really remember."

"You'd remember if you'd ever seen his back," Paul said with some irony. He gave her a quick glance. "I don't think you ever have."

Rita looked at him in astonishment. "Now that you make a point of it, I don't believe I have. Helen wears a bathing suit and takes the children in the lake, but Bill generally comes in slacks and sports shirt and sits on the beach."

"I thought so," Paul said. "His back is a mess. He wouldn't want to expose it on a public beach."

Rita frowned. "It's that bad?"

"That bad," Paul said, as they came to the intersection and he brought the car to a stop for a moment. He looked at her with a solemn expression. "I've seen many scars in my time, but none any worse than his. It seems he was both crushed and burned in that car crash. He's lucky he lived and was able to walk again."

"Would he have had major surgery?"

"That and some plastic work as well," Paul said, starting the car again and heading out into traffic. "And it's my guess something has gone wrong."

"You mean something has developed from the original surgery?" she said.

"It's pressure on a nerve or group of nerves," he told her, his eyes fixed on the road ahead again. "It could be caused by any number of things. It might even be some sort of tumor. There has been plenty of time for a growth to develop."

Rita sensed his concern. "It could really be bad, then?"

"I'd say it is bad at this minute. To help him, it's necessary to get the X-rays and records of the work done on him at the time of the accident. At least having them would save a lot of time and guesswork." He paused. "In the meantime, I'll check him thoroughly if he comes to the office."

"But you doubt that he will."

Paul sighed. "I don't understand his behavior at all. It's not normal. I used to like Bill, but now I'm beginning to wonder if I know him at all."

"So am I," Rita said slowly. "And, I'm afraid, so is Helen."

He took his eyes from the road for a second to flash her an angry look. "And your strange remarks aren't making the picture any clearer."

"All right." She sat back against the seat cushions with a deep sigh. "I'll tell you what I know. But it's strictly in confidence."

When she finished, Paul gave a low whistle. "A fine kettle of fish," he said.

Rita looked at him. "You don't think he could be some kind of criminal? That he did some awful thing in California and then changed his name and came here to hide?"

Paul sighed. "He couldn't have chosen a better place. Riverdale is pretty remote."

"I can't believe it of Bill," she argued. "I can't see him hurting anyone. I can't even picture him as a robber."

"Think it over," he said in a cynical voice. "How often have you read of cases where men who've changed their names have been both thieves and killers? And almost invariably their neighbors have thought them fine, upstanding citizens."

She nodded. "I know. It frightens me. They're usually quiet and reserved like Bill."

They swung around a corner and started down the road that led to the river and the country club.

Paul headed the car into the country club parking lot and found an empty space in the back row of cars. There must have been more than a hundred cars parked in front of the imposing white building that housed the club. It was three stories high and of Colonial styling, with a tall cupola structure painted gold. This towered above the surrounding area and was a landmark and a source of pride.

The club was built directly on the river bank, and below it were the wharves and boathouses.

The five-piece orchestra was already playing when they entered the big main room where the special functions and dances were held. It had been recently rebuilt, and the walls were done in walnut panels, with a corner bar at one end and a platform for the orchestra directly opposite. There was a balcony facing the river and doors leading to it from the dance floor. This offered a pleasant place to cool off between dances on a hot summer evening such as this. And many romantic young couples spent most of their time at some isolated spot along the balcony that extended the full length of the building.

A cut-out of an anchor and a large reproduction of the club emblem decorated the wall nearest the entrance. The dining room was on an upper floor reached by a wide stairway, and there were executive rooms at this level and on the third floor as well.

The lights in the ballroom had been dimmed, and there were a number of couples on the floor dancing to the strains of a lively foxtrot played by the orchestra. There were also the usual number of couples clustered around the bar and keeping the two barmen moving at a lively pace.

Paul and Rita avoided the drinking crowd as much as possible and usually spent most of the evening on the dance floor or out on the balcony.

He smiled at her. "We might as well enjoy this," he said. And they joined the other dancers.

As they passed the bar for perhaps the fifth time while circling around the floor, Rita found herself staring almost directly into Cliff Thomson's arrogant face. The big man smiled broadly, and she was glad that Paul made a turn on the floor so she was whisked away.

She told Paul: "We have a friend here to-night."

"A lot of them, I imagine," he said, looking down at her. "Who?"

"Cliff."

"Great!" Paul said with a groan. "That's all we need."

"If we keep away from the bar we should be all right," Rita said. "That's where he'll spend most of the night."

The music ended, and they applauded with the others. The orchestra settled down to an encore. And when the music finished this time, they were on the other side of the room from the bar. They were just about to go out on the balcony when a familiar voice rang out behind them.

"Paul, just a minute!" They turned and saw Dr. Jonas Arbo.

The tall thin man looked quite suave and handsome in his white dinner jacket. The dance was formal, although the women usually wore cocktail length dresses for summer occasions.

"I want to get a bit of information from you," Dr. Arbo told Paul. And he smiled at the pleasant, gray-haired woman who'd been dancing with him. "Mrs. Wilson and Rita won't mind exchanging a little gossip for a minute, I'm sure."

Rita laughed. "Just don't be too long," she warned. "I know you doctors when you begin talking shop."

Dr. Arbo raised a hand. "I won't keep him more than a few minutes." And the two men went out on the balcony.

Mrs. Wilson was a widow who had been a friend of Rita's parents. After the usual polite inquiries had been exchanged, there was little for them to talk about. The music started again, and Rita glanced impatiently toward the balcony, hoping Paul would return and rescue her.

"This is our dance, isn't it?" It was Cliff Thomson, who'd come up on them quietly and now waited for Rita to join him on the floor.

She looked into the assured, arrogant face with startled eyes and protested. "No," she said, "Paul is coming right back."

"He may be longer than you think," Cliff said mockingly. And with a brash smile for Mrs. Wilson: "I'm sure this good lady won't mind my stealing you for a few minutes."

Rita turned pleading eyes to the older woman, but Mrs. Wilson just gave them a glassy stare, smiled and nodded her approval. It was all Cliff needed. He took the still protesting Rita in his arms and swung her out on the floor.

When the music ended, Rita saw Paul striding across the broad floor to rescue her with a grim expression on his stern, young face. Now she was seized with a new worry. She didn't want Paul to flatten Cliff right in the middle of Riverdale's social set. And she knew he was capable of it in his present mood. As he came up to them, she gave him a placating smile.

"Cliff saved me from missing some wonderful music," she said.

Paul's eyes narrowed as he glanced from her to the slightly uneasy Cliff. "You really enjoyed yourself?" he asked.

"Oh, yes," Rita said. "Cliff's a remarkable dancer."

The big man seemed to accept this at face value. He chuckled and told Paul: "We used to do a lot of this in the old days. Why don't you two come over to our place after they close here? We've got a crowd coming, and Sue would be glad to have you."

"Thanks," Paul said coldly. "We can't make it. I have some early calls to look after in the morning."

Cliff was apparently determined not to be insulted. He waved a hamlike hand in a gesture of resignation, and his broad face continued to wear the same arrogant smile. "Another week, Doc. You're both always welcome." Then he went back to join the group at the bar.

"What kept you so long with Dr. Arbo?" Rita asked.

"I've been given a briefing about what has been going on behind the scenes with the board," Paul said. "Arbo has a cousin on the council and got his information first hand. They've got a scheme afoot to get rid of Mary Grant before she even gets here."

"That must be what Cliff was talking about," Rita said. They took a stand at the balcony railing, and Paul listened while she told him what had been said.

When she finished, he stared out at the calm water of the river, now given a silver sheen by a pale three-quarter moon. He was silent for a moment; then he said: "We're headed for trouble. No doubt about that."

The next few days were uneventful. Bill Ferguson went back to work on Monday, but he did not keep his appointment to visit Paul at his office. Grace Thomas began to show a slight response to the drug Dr. Solomon was trying on her, and Dr. Arbo warned Mrs. Galway she would be able to leave the hospital in a few days. Neither Rita nor Mrs. Galway was pleased at this news.

From the moment the older woman had

transferred to Grace Thomas' room, there had been an improvement in the desperately ill girl's state of mind. Rita feared there would be a relapse in her general condition once Mrs. Galway left. She worried about this for days prior to the diabetic woman's discharge.

Then, toward the end of the week, she had an unexpected opportunity to talk with Mrs. Roger Barry. The specialist from Boston had visited her and stayed for a second day. According to the word that leaked downstairs, Ellen May Barry was feeling much better. She was taking a special course of tranquillizers prescribed by the eminent Boston doctor and responding well to them. The private nurse was not so strict about others on the staff entering her patient's room, and on this particular day, when Rita was upstairs collecting her reports, she noticed the door was open. Ellen May Barry was seated in an easy chair, reading.

On impulse Rita paused a fraction of a moment outside the door and, realizing this might be her only opportunity to talk directly with her, knocked gently on the door frame.

Ellen May Barry glanced up from her book. "Yes, Nurse?" she said.

Rita stepped into the room and said: "I'm Rita Lewis. I don't suppose you remember me. But you rescued me during a snowball battle one day."

Ellen May stared at her curiously for a second, and then a light of recognition appeared in her eyes. She smiled. "Of course I remember you," she said. "We used to meet quite often before your family moved away. I heard you were a nurse and back here."

"I've wanted to speak to you," Rita said. "But you were too ill."

The young woman's face clouded. A delicate hand smoothed the pages of her open book, and she glanced down. "Yes. I feel better now."

"I've often thought about you and the good times we had," Rita said.

Ellen May looked up, and some of the brightness returned to her face. "They were wonderful days!" She sighed. "So far away now." She studied Rita closely. "You look so well, so alert and happy! But of course you must enjoy your work here. What a marvelous thing to be of service, really to be of some use."

Rita shrugged. "I do enjoy my work. But that's what it is — a job. I think most people find a niche and play their parts in life."

"Don't think everyone is so fortunate," Ellen May Barry warned her with a sigh. "There are people who see their lives slipping by pointlessly and are helpless to do anything about it but count the days, the weeks, the years!"

Rita said: "I don't want to try cheering you up with mealy-mouthed phrases, but in many ways you are a very lucky person."

Ellen May regarded her with a cynical smile. "No, I don't think advice or philosophy would have too much weight, coming from the little girl I rescued from the snowballers."

Rita laughed. "I was going to say life and good health are precious gifts. We should put them to good use."

Ellen May raised her eyebrows. "Some of us are too weak to do that. We find it easier just to drift."

"But a pattern can be changed," Rita insisted. "I think we can build a way of life just as we exercise muscles to make them strong. One decision made, one worthwhile thing accomplished, and the will grows stronger."

The woman in the chair closed her book. "You always were a curious little girl," she said with amused interest. "I'm pleased to find out you haven't changed."

Rita still had a complex dating back to the days when Ellen May had been the older girl.

"I shouldn't really be here at all," she admitted. "And I suppose I am presumptuous."

"I wish you'd come more often," Ellen May said quietly. Her eyes met Rita's, and she went on hesitantly: "I guess you know why I'm here and the condition I was in when I came." She paused. "I thought I didn't want to live. I know better now. Life has value, no matter how bitter."

"That is so true," Rita said. And then, in a rush of words, she told the story of Grace Thomas on the third floor; Grace Thomas, who asked only for life and who soon must die.

Ellen May listened with a slight frown. "But there must be something," she said, "something that can be done."

"Not from a medical standpoint," Rita told her. And then she went on to talk about Mrs. Galway and the wonders she'd worked for the sick girl.

When she'd finished, Ellen May Barry looked at her with new excitement in her eyes. She said: "Do you think that girl would let me move in with her when Mrs. Galway goes?"

As first Rita was startled. "But you have a private room with your own nurse!"

"Do you think she would," Ellen May repeated, "if I wanted to very badly."

Rita smiled her gratitude. "I think it would be a wonderful thing for you to do," she said quietly.

Chapter Nine

The next ten days passed at a rapid pace. The warm summer weather remained unbroken except for an occasional thunderstorm. Perhaps the thing that had stirred the hospital most, other than the arrival of Dr. Mary Grant to take over, had been the transfer of Ellen May Barry from her private room on the second floor to share the semi-private on the third with Grace Thomas.

No one had been more surprised than the sad-faced Dr. Solomon who was physician to them both. He had come to Rita's desk on the day Ellen May told him of her plans and expressed his complete astonishment.

"A most unusual request," he told Rita with a shake of his iron-gray head. "I hardly knew how to answer."

Rita smiled. "You won't get any complaints from this department. We can use Mrs. Barry's room."

"I know that," Dr. Solomon agreed. "But

as you are aware, Mrs. Barry has been a most difficult patient up to now."

"She's very nice, really," Rita said. "And I think she'll do Grace Thomas a lot of good now that Mrs. Galway's going."

Dr. Solomon shrugged. "I won't deny I consider it a blessing. But I'm still baffled as to how it came about."

She laughed. "Why not accept it and ask no questions?"

He nodded. "That is what I must do. Indeed, you're quite right." And he went on his way.

The two women became friends at first meeting. And since Ellen May Barry was not physically ill, she was able to give a good deal of time and assistance to the desperately sick Grace. The only thing marring the happy situation was another relapse on the sick girl's part. In spite of all Dr. Solomon's efforts, she seemed to be steadily fading away.

Her husband noticed it as soon as he returned to the hospital from his period of duty. He invited Rita to have lunch with him in the cafeteria and confided his fears.

"She's worse," he told Rita across the table. "I can see it. The drug doesn't seem to be helping any more."

"That's often the pattern," she said. "Undoubtedly Dr. Solomon will switch to something else."

The young naval officer's face was drawn. "And if that fails?"

Rita's eyes met his. "Don't get panicky. Don't let your fears take hold of you this way. She'll sense it, and you have no right to rob her of hope."

Jack Thomas looked down contritely. "I guess I do almost everything the wrong way. All I ever think of is myself."

"That's not true either," she said in a more gentle tone. "But ever since you've known what you two are facing, you must have been prepared for this. Now the time has come for you to play your part. You can make it easier or harder for her."

He looked at her with admiration showing plainly in his eyes. "I don't know what I'd do without you," he said. "You have no idea what it means having someone to talk to, to advise me as you do."

She shrugged. "It's part of my work."

"Not to this extent," he said. "You're doing this for us. And on your own."

Of course he was right. Even though she didn't want to admit it, she had become involved in this case.

"I won't be testing for a while," he said. "They have the submarine in the shipyard again for some new fitting. I should be able to get up here more often. I want to spend all the time I can with her."

"I know," Rita agreed quietly.

"That Mrs. Barry is as nice with her as Mrs. Galway was," Jack Thomas went on. "It was surely good luck that she decided to share Grace's room."

Rita nodded. "Yes. I think so."

He looked at her with puzzled eyes. "Kind of strange, too. I hear she has plenty of money and had a private room and nurse on the second floor. Wonder what made her change her mind?"

"I imagine she became lonesome," Rita said. "I'm sure being with Grace is good for her."

And of course this was the way it turned out. Ellen May Barry suddenly seemed to blossom. There was a new urgency and purpose about her concern for her seriously ill roommate that outdid that shown by Mrs. Galway.

Dr. Solomon confided in Rita that the wealthy young matron had talked to him privately about Grace's treatments. She had insisted he let her call in some outside specialists in the field until he showed her the complete correspondence he'd had with several clinics on the case and convinced her

144

that everything possible was being done. Then she had asked that he try to locate other and more potent drugs being used for the disease on an experimental basis. Expense was no object. She couldn't accept the simple fact that Grace had to lose her life.

Dr. Solomon smiled wryly. "It is rather ironical," he said, "to discover Mrs. Barry putting such a premium on life, when she came here because she had so little regard for her own."

Even the elderly, distinguished-looking Roger Barry showed less tendency to stiffness when he visited the hospital. Because Ellen May was mingling freely with other patients on her floor and generally making herself useful, he seemed to be much more at ease. Rita saw him in conversation with Dr. Francis in the lobby, and there was actually a smile on his bloated, purplish face. She thought he must have been handsome at one time, and she could sense there was new hope in him.

Then the weather changed abruptly. After the long weeks of almost unbroken sunlight, it started to rain. And day after day it was dark, with a continuous light drizzle or else a series of heavy showers.

It was Monday again. And because of the

weather, Rita had spent a quiet weekend catching up with work and doing some reading.

Superintendent of Nurses Laura Graham rose from her desk and went to the window. "There's no halfway about it," she said, staring out with a doleful look on her pale face. "Either the sun is blazing or we have a flood."

Rita looked up from her typewriter. "Not the ideal way to begin a week."

"Nor for Dr. Mary Grant to start her work here," Laura Graham said with a smile as she returned to her post.

"I wonder if she's here yet," Rita said. "I mean in the building."

"I haven't any idea," Laura Graham told her in a weary voice as she drew a bulging correspondence file from the top right desk drawer and set it before her. "But you'll know when she is. All the men will be running after her!"

It was only a few minutes later that Dr. Jonas Arbo made an entrance in the room, his thin old face wearing a broad grin. He stopped before Rita's desk and announced: "She's here!"

Laura Graham glanced up at him grimly and then turned to Rita. "Didn't I tell you!"

She laughed, and Dr. Arbo looked puzzled. "Some kind of joke?" he asked.

"You wouldn't enjoy it," Laura Graham said. "What's she like?"

"Dr. Mary Grant is the sort of woman I would marry if I were thirty years younger," he said importantly.

"What a tragedy for her she arrived so late," Laura Graham said with smiling sarcasm. "I asked for information, not bragging!"

"She's a lovely girl," Dr. Arbo said. "But you'll see her soon. She and Dr. Francis are going to make the rounds." He paused. "But that's not why I'm here."

"Lovely," Laura Graham said. "Why are you here?"

"My business is with Miss Lewis," the bald-headed old man said with dignity. He smiled at Rita. "I'm in need of the usual. Private room for an emergency operation I'm doing tomorrow."

"If it's an emergency, I can look after you," she said.

"It's an emergency all right," he said. "Both the patient and I have been postponing action for some time. Now I'm worried. It's young Mrs. Miller. They have her full name and address at the business office. You may know her. Her husband works for

147

the pulp mill, and she comes to the country club dances once in a while."

"I think I do," she said, recalling a small blonde woman who laughed a lot.

"It's endometriosis," he said. "She's been having repeated attacks of pain. This time it's severe. I'd like to bring her in this afternoon and operate in the morning."

"That will be all right," Rita promised.

"There is a cyst involved," he went on with a worried expression. "I'm not sure about the size or how extensive the operation may have to be."

"Well, at least most cysts of that type aren't malignant," she said.

"True," he agreed. "But you can't ever be one hundred percent sure. It's the exceptions you have to be on guard for. That's why I don't want to postpone this another day."

Laura Graham spoke up. "She won't need a private duty nurse, I hope. We haven't one on call. A lot of them are on vacation."

The thin man shook his head. "No. She won't want private duty attention." And to Rita: "You can count on her needing a bed for seven to ten days."

"It may have to be a semi-private," she told him.

"Do the best you can," Dr. Arbo said. "I'll leave it with you."

After he'd left, Rita called the business office, got the full information on Mrs. Miller and arranged for a bed in a third floor room. There had been no easing in the pressure for admissions. And in view of the number of operations scheduled and the steady flow of other patients, it didn't seem that there would be. Some people apparently waited for the warm weather and the holiday period for surgery which had no urgency. In a way she agreed with them. It was more pleasant to go through the usual period of invalidism in the summer when it was warm enough to sit outside.

She had just finished a phone call concerning another patient and was preparing to do some more typing on her lists when she heard voices from the doorway. When she raised her eyes, she saw Dr. Francis and a rather stunning young woman at his side. She did not need to be told that this must be Dr. Mary Grant.

Dr. Francis came forward with one of his prim smiles. "And this is our front office nurse for the day shift," he told the woman, "Miss Rita Lewis. Miss Lewis, this is Dr. Mary Grant."

Rita rose to greet the new superintendent, but Mary Grant waved her back to her chair with a graceful hand motion. "Please," she said, "don't let me interrupt." She was slim, and wore a two-piece, smartly cut summer suit of some material with a dark pencil stripe that emphasized her attractive figure. Her hair was dark brown and worn shoulder length. It framed an intelligent, even-featured face that showed strength. Yet there was an expression of kindness and good humor in the large gray eyes.

She asked: "What time do you take care of the floor reports?"

"I usually leave just after two," Rita said.

Dr. Mary Grant nodded. "That seems as good a time as any. Do you have to rush to complete your files?"

"No. It seems to give me enough time." It was apparent by her questions the young woman doctor knew her work.

Mary Grant glanced around the room. "It's a good size," she said. "I like plenty of space to work in."

Dr. Francis laughed politely. "Then you'll hardly be satisfied with my office. I consider it cramped." He nodded to Laura Graham's desk. "The superintendent of nurses also shares this room."

"I see," Dr. Mary Grant said. "In that case, you haven't more than enough space."

"Most of our offices are on the small side," Dr. Francis said, frowning slightly.

"But I think you'll agree we do have good large rooms for the patients and an excellent main operating room."

"I'm very much impressed with your upstairs facilities," Dr. Mary Grant agreed with him. Then, turning to Rita with a warm smile, she continued: "I don't imagine you're ever satisfied with the number of rooms, Miss Lewis."

She returned the smile. "Not ever. We've had an amazing number of admissions this year."

"The growing population," Dr. Mary Grant said, a twinkle showing in the gray eyes again. "But in a sense, you're fortunate. Some privately endowed hospitals are having problems today, especially in the very small towns. Patients are tending to go to larger centers and clinics for medical attention these days."

Dr. Francis rubbed his hands together lightly and gave another of his polite laughs. "Well, we are fortunate in having no close competitors."

"You really are," Dr. Mary Grant emphasized the point. "In Maine that was one of our problems. There were two other small hospitals in towns nearby. And of course each town was full of its own importance and supported only the local hospital. It meant that a thinly populated area was divided by three, and there were a lot of beds empty much of the time, with corresponding deficits for each hospital."

"A condition not appreciated by the taxpayers and the local councils," Dr. Francis said.

"Exactly," Mary Grant agreed. And then: "What is the attitude of the town council here? Do they show much interest."

The precise head doctor didn't blink an eye. "I would say they showed a great deal of interest, Dr. Grant," he said smoothly.

Rita wondered if the young woman doctor had any idea of the innuendo contained in Dr. Francis' seemingly innocent remark. She guessed not. But it wouldn't be long until she found out the true picture of things in Riverdale.

Dr. Grant smiled at her. "Nice meeting you, Miss Lewis. I'm sure I'll enjoy working with you." And with this she and Dr. Francis made their way to the door. They met Laura Graham on the way in, and this meant a slight delay while further introductions were made and a few polite remarks made. Then the two doctors vanished down the corridor.

Laura Graham glanced after them and came into the office. "My timing was just right," the older nurse said. "What do you think of her?"

"She seems competent," Rita said.

Laura Graham sat at her desk. "She's too attractive, if you ask me. A girl doesn't want that kind of good looks if she plans an executive career."

"I don't know." Rita laughed. "It might help."

"With the men, of course," Laura Graham conceded. "Not with the women. You wait and see!"

Chapter Ten

Another week passed. Each time that Rita questioned Dr. Solomon about Grace Thomas, he was either outright gloomy or evasive. And the reports she received from Ellen May Barry were not much brighter. Ellen May had lingered on, sharing the room with the sick girl; Rita suspected she would have otherwise been discharged by Dr. Solomon.

The weather had changed again, and it was warm and fine. Jack Thomas was due back in the afternoon from a test run of the new atomic submarine, *Alcestis*. Rita found it necessary to go to the third floor to check on some conflicting entries in one of dour Augusta Adair's reports. When she stepped off the elevator, she met Dr. Solomon.

The veteran doctor gave her one of his rare smiles. "We don't often see you on the floor at this time of day," he said.

"Some extra detail work," she explained, holding up the file she'd brought along with her. And then she asked the usual question: "How is Grace Thomas today?"

Dr. Solomon's gloomy face became even more gloomy. "She's slipping away," he said. "There is no other word to describe it."

"None of the drugs have helped?" Rita asked.

"She proved allergic to one, the most hopeful one in fact, and we had to take her off it," the old doctor said. "I'm expecting another one in a day or so. We'll try it."

"Her husband should be back this afternoon," Rita told him.

"I'm glad to hear that," Dr. Solomon said. "It's too bad he's stationed so far away and has so much duty time. He's losing precious hours with her."

"He feels that, too," she said. "Perhaps he should ask for some kind of leave. But I know his branch of the engineering department has been very busy with these tests."

"Ask him to phone me when he comes, please," the old doctor said. "If it weren't for Mrs. Barry, I don't know what that poor girl would do."

"And don't you think she has helped Mrs. Barry as well?"

Dr. Solomon gave her a meaningful look.

"The change in that woman has been simply unbelievable." And with a parting nod, he moved down the corridor.

Dour Augusta Adair was waiting at her desk to battle for her rights. According to her, she'd made no mistake. However, it took Rita only a few minutes to show her where the entries varied and have her admit she had done one of them wrong.

Rita put the file back under her arm. "We have that settled," she said.

The head nurse scowled. "If I hadn't to do a half-dozen jobs, I wouldn't make mistakes. And that wasn't a bad one."

Rita smiled. "We get them from every floor."

Augusta Adair bridled. "You'll get more of them once Miss Know-It-All takes over. I hear she's talking about changing the day shift from seven to three and making it from eight to four. She can count me out if she does! It would mean driving in the thick of traffic every day."

"It wouldn't really be so awful, would it?" Rita questioned. "Riverdale is not a big city."

"The mill crowd comes and goes at those same hours, and you'd catch all that traffic," the dour woman complained. And then, with an appraising glance at Rita, she continued: "I hear your boyfriend is sweet on her. A neighbor of mine saw him out driving with Dr. Grant."

Rita tried to sound casual. "They've known each other for some time."

"Better watch your step," Augusta Adair commented dryly.

"I'm not worried in the least," Rita told the head nurse. But as she walked down the corridor toward Grace's room, she admitted to herself she was worried.

When she entered Grace's room, Ellen May Barry was reading to her from a leading woman's magazine. The sick girl's face brightened as Rita entered, and Ellen May closed the magazine and stood up.

"What a wonderful surprise!" Grace said, holding out a thin hand for Rita to take. "I've been thinking about you and not expecting you until this afternoon. And it seemed such a long time away."

Rita sat on her bed and took the emaciated hand in her own. "Someone made a mistake." Rita smiled. "So I had an excuse to roam around."

Ellen May Barry smiled from the other side of the bed. "Which reminds me I should do some roaming myself," she said. "I promised Mrs. Miller in 320 I'd look in on her this morning. I'll go now."

157

After she'd gone, Grace told Rita: "She's been awfully good to me."

"I'm sure you've helped each other."

Grace's wan face brightened. "And Mrs. Galway came in the other day. She generally gets here twice a week."

"And your husband will be here this afternoon," Rita said gently.

"Jack!" The sick girl's eyes took on a tiny sparkle. "He's always so good for me. He'll probably pick up Mother and bring her as well. I haven't seen her since he brought her before. She's so crippled. But we talk on the phone every day."

"It would be nice if Jack could stay a few days this time," Rita said.

"I'd like that," Grace agreed with a deep sigh. "I worry about him on that submarine. I'm not sure these test runs they make are safe."

Rita laughed. "He's probably a lot better off than driving a car."

The girl in the bed shivered. "I'd like to believe that. But these new atomic submarines dive so deep. If anything happened down there in the darkness —"

"You mustn't think about such things," Rita said. "You want to cheer Jack up when he comes; not worry him."

"He worries too much," Grace admitted.

"Worries about me and whether the doctors are doing the right thing." She shook her head on the pillow, and Rita was afraid she might be going to cry. "It seems so unfair! We had such a short time before all this happened."

"Don't feel that way," Rita told her. "I've come to understand Jack well enough to know he'd rather have things as they are than not ever to have met you. You should be happy. You have a husband who loves you very deeply."

"I know," the girl said. "And that sustains me. The rest doesn't matter, does it? It has been so wonderful. And I can't really complain that it's coming to an cnd. Everything ends, even the most perfect love. And many people aren't as lucky as we. The dream is destroyed before the end. That can't happen with Jack and me."

"Not with Jack and you," Rita echoed her sentiment in a quiet tone. "Never."

Ellen May came back, and Rita left, promising to see Grace again later. Because of an extra heavy day, she didn't go back to the room that afternoon. But she did see Jack in the lobby and talked to him for a moment. By coincidence, he did have a few days' leave, and she told him to be sure and phone Dr. Solomon.

That evening Grace went into a coma. Two days later she died. The news of her death saddened everyone in the hospital, especially Ellen May Barry. The wealthy young matron kept the long death vigil at her friend's bedside with Jack. And when it was over and she was alone in the room, she called Dr. Solomon and told him she was leaving the hospital. She was gone by that evening.

Rita saw her at the funeral. She was one of the last to leave the graveside on the warm summer afternoon of Grace's burial in a quiet cemetery not far from Riverdale. Rita also noted that Ellen May Barry's husband was with her. She thought that the elderly Roger Barry looked pale and troubled, but she had no opportunity to speak with either of them.

That evening she had an unexpected visitor. She was reading on the verandah when the big limousine hesitated and then came to a stop on the road by her driveway. A man got out of the car and came around to walk up to the house. He was wearing a dark suit and white shirt and tie. He was halfway to the verandah before she recognized him as Roger Barry.

The big man with the white hair and distinguished face stopped and looked up at her soberly. "I trust I'm not intruding, Miss Lewis. I made up my mind to call on you rather suddenly. I should have phoned before I came."

"It doesn't matter," she said with a faint smile, "as long as you don't mind finding me in these old slacks. Won't you come in?"

Roger Barry nodded. "Thank you, Miss Lewis." He came up the stairs and followed her inside. When they were seated across from one another in the living room, he said: "First, I've come to thank you, Miss Lewis, for the kindness you've done my wife and me."

"I don't understand," Rita said.

"I think you do," the elderly man said, looking at her solemnly. "I know it was your doing that she came to be with Mrs. Thomas. What those weeks have done for her!" He sighed. "When Grace Thomas died, I was afraid it might all end, that the gains we'd made would be lost." His eyes met hers. "Now I'm beginning to hope this may not be true. Ellen May and I had a long talk after the funeral this afternoon. And I found myself extending her a belatedly generous offer."

He stopped for a moment as if he found the next words too difficult to utter. Rita found herself feeling sorry for the man.

She said: "You don't have to tell me any of this, Mr. Barry."

"But I want to," he insisted. "Today I offered Ellen May what I should have several years ago if I'd been fair. I told her she could have her freedom without any opposition on my part. She had made it plain many times in the past it was what she wanted." He paused again. "And what do you think happened?"

"I have no idea," Rita said.

"She refused it, Miss Lewis," Roger Barry said earnestly. He glanced down. "You have no idea, no conception at all, what that meant to me."

"Ellen May is a rather wonderful person," Rita said. "She has a habit of rescuing people." And she smiled.

Roger Barry returned the smile. "Yes. I've heard about your predicament when you were left alone to battle the boys in that snowball fight. Well, this time Ellen May is taking on a somewhat bigger task than she did that day she helped you, but I have no doubt she'll come through with the same sort of victory. She's making plans already, and that new Dr. Grant is encouraging her. Riverdale has never had a Woman's Hospital Aid group, and Ellen May wants to organize one before anyone else gets the idea."

"And we need the help so badly," Rita said, delighted at the news. "I think she'll be ideal for the work."

"So do I," Roger Barry said, and stood up. "For the first time in a long while I'm proud of my marriage and my wife. I've always loved her, but I've never been really aware of her possibilities. And I owe a great deal of this to you."

"You're wrong about that," Rita protested.

Roger Barry walked slowly toward the door. "No matter what you say, I know the facts." He faced her. "And there was nothing less I could do than come here and express my heartfelt thanks."

Long after he had gone, Rita sat out on the verandah, thinking.

Grace was gone. But she had left them all a little richer. And she would live on in beauty in their memories. Now that Ellen May Barry had become aware of her own capabilities for good, she would go on to find her place in the order of things. Rita was not worried about her. It would be different for Jack Thomas. The young widower would have to find a new life for himself. But he did have the advantage of youth, and while he was badly hurt now, time would eventually heal his wounds.

A few days later she had lunch with the

young naval officer before he returned to Portsmouth and his submarine testing duties. She smiled at him across the table.

"These luncheons together have become a pleasant habit," she said. "Please do come back. I'll miss you."

"I'd like to," he said gravely, "if I may." He glanced around the busy room. "I don't suppose you'll understand what I mean. But there's something of her here in the hospital. I've grown so used to coming here and seeing her. I guess I'll always think she's in that upstairs room waiting."

"I understand," she said.

"So coming back will seem a natural thing," he said awkwardly.

"Just don't look backward," she said. "She wouldn't want that. It was a thing she rarely did herself."

Jack Thomas stared at her in wonder. "It often amazes me," he said, "how well you came to know her in such a short time."

"Often when there isn't much time, emotions intensify," she said. "She'll always be very vivid in my memories."

Jack said goodbye and promised he'd be up for another weekend before the month was over. He planned to spend a few days with Grace's mother, and he would also come to see Rita at the hospital.

So it was back to routine again.

A few of the staff deliberately tried to cause problems for Dr. Grant, but most were willing to do their best and see how she managed. Of course Dr. Paul Reid did a lot of missionary work for her and gave much of his time to helping her; so much, indeed, that Rita began to feel she was being neglected and told him so.

They had gone to Scarboro for one of their regular drives and were now seated in a booth at the roadside restaurant, enjoying the boisterous activities of a teen-age group seated at the soda counter.

Paul looked at her with a smile. "You're very quiet and sober tonight," he said.

She shook her head. "I don't think any more so than usual."

"I do," he insisted.

Rita gave him a teasing look. "Perhaps it's because you're used to gayer company lately."

He nodded. "I know what you're hinting. You think I've been seeing too much of Dr. Mary Grant."

She shrugged. "Well, since you read my mind, there's no point in my saying anything."

"I can read your mind on that subject," he said with a slight frown. "Whenever I've

165

been with Mary, it's been strictly hospital business."

"Still, she is charming."

"Agreed."

"And you do like her," she said.

"Agreed again," he said. "But that's a long way from either of us being madly in love."

She studied him carefully. "I don't know, Paul," she said at last. "I honestly don't know. And if you want to be truthful, it's my guess you don't either."

He laughed awkwardly. "That's crazy talk. All I'm trying to do is help the girl. You know the board are after her."

"Are they?" she said. "I've only heard rumors. I've seen no signs of action."

"Give them a chance, and you will soon enough," he told her grimly.

She smiled. "Maybe that's all a bogey you're conjuring to justify what you're doing."

"Is your friend Cliff Thomson a sham bogey?" Paul questioned sharply. "You know how he's been talking lately."

Rita had to admit this was true. But she still believed Paul was being more attentive to the lady doctor than the situation required. "I'm still not convinced of the urgency of it all," she said.

"When it comes to that," he told her indignantly, "what about you and Jack Thomas? You tell me he's coming up here again soon. And he has no wife in hospital now."

"That's different," she said.

"I don't see anything different about it now that he's free," Paul hammered the point.

"Perhaps we'd better drop the subject." Rita smiled. "We'll never agree, so that's the simplest way."

They talked of other things for the balance of the evening together, and when Paul kissed her good night it was almost like before.

Towards the end of August there was a slowing down of surgical cases. And since this was not a time when the hospital was besieged with other patients, Rita found herself with a lot less work to do. There were actually a number of beds going begging. It was a happy experience, and she had no thought of complaining. She only wondered if this might be the lull before the storm.

One day Dr. Jonas made one of his frequent appearances in the office. "I'm bringing in a child with Hirschsprung's disease the day after tomorrow. We'll be operating the following morning. I know there are plenty of beds, but I wanted to mention it. You can get the details from the business office."

Rita made a note of it. "I'll look after it," she said. "What exactly is the condition?"

"It requires a colectomy," Dr. Arbo explained, "the removal of a constricted loop of bowel and then joining the bowel above and below. It's a nasty enough bit of work. I'm having Dr. Reid do the operation, and I'm assisting. It will take at least two hours and could run as long as five."

"That sounds major," she said. "You'll need specials for afterward, won't you?"

"That's right."

"I'll try to line them up," she said. "I'm doubling with Laura's work while she's on vacation. What causes this type of trouble?"

Dr. Arbo rubbed his chin. "It's not caused. It's a condition of the large bowel present from birth. You see it most often in males, and it only turns up in about one in ten thousand cases. The operation is both major and serious, but today well over ninety percent of the cases are cured."

"That sounds hopeful, anyway."

He nodded. "There's another thing worrying me these days. I've been reading about quite a few hospitals in New England having epidemics of staph infection. I hope it doesn't get this far."

Rita frowned. "But isn't it caused mostly by bad sterile conditions?"

"Not always," Dr. Arbo said. "Every once in a while it seems to get in the air, and you're in trouble. Just cross your fingers we don't ever have the problem. I've been through one siege of it, and that was enough."

She sighed. "Well, the really warm weather is all over."

"Weather hasn't anything to do with it," the old doctor said. "I can think of times when it hit a hospital in mid-winter." He sighed and walked out and down the corridor.

Rita was about to leave the office and go to the floors for the day's reports when the phone rang. She answered it, and the voice at the other end of the line was familiar.

"Rita, I've been trying to reach you!" It was Helen Ferguson, and her voice was strained.

Rita sensed an emergency and at once thought of the children. "What is it?" she asked.

"Bill," Helen said brokenly. "He's on his way to the hospital now. He collapsed at the office a few minutes ago."

"I'll look out for him," Rita promised. "Now don't worry!"

"I can't help it." Helen was crying now. "We all knew this was coming, but he wouldn't listen! He wouldn't listen!"

"Are you planning to come right away?" she asked.

"As soon as a taxi can get here," Helen said. "I'll stop by Mother's and leave the girls."

"Don't let yourself get all upset," Rita cautioned her. "Did they tell you anything about what happened at the office?"

"No," Helen protested tearfully. "But I know. It's the pain. He's been having it more often lately. It probably hit him, and he passed out."

"Well, perhaps it's for the best," Rita said, striving to find some small seed of comfort for the stricken woman. "At least now he'll get looked after."

"You'll still be there on duty when I get there, won't you?" Helen asked.

"Naturally," Rita said. "I wouldn't think of leaving until everything is all right."

"Do what you can for him, Rita," Helen pleaded before she hung up.

Rita put down the phone, her pretty face shadowed with concern. So it had finally happened.

She wondered if Paul might still be in the building and was on her way to the lobby when she heard the scream of the ambulance's siren as it came down Main Street toward the hospital.

Chapter Eleven

A wan Bill Ferguson was stretched out in bed with Paul Reid, Rita and Helen grouped around it. The sick man glanced about the small private room and said: "This is the last thing I need. I feel well enough to go home now."

Paul gave him a reproving look. "And keel over again as you did at the office?"

"That was just the heat," Bill argued wearily. And with an appealing glance in his wife's direction: "It's nonsense my staying here."

Helen was pale but firm. "I don't want to hear another word from you, Bill," she said. "You're in the hospital, and here you're going to stay until they've taken the proper X-rays and made the right tests and found out what's wrong."

Rita felt she could express her own convictions. "She's right, Bill. And this time you've got to do as she says."

Bill closed his eyes and groaned. "Let a

man get off his feet just for a minute, and you women down him!"

Paul gave Rita a meaningful glance and then turned his attention to Bill again. He said: "Bill, I've seen your back, and I know your trouble more or less stems from the old injury. Now before we go much further, I want to get your plates and case history from San Francisco."

The man on the bed opened his eyes and frowned at the young doctor. "What do you need them for? You're a doctor. You should be able to diagnose me."

"Why make things more difficult?" Paul asked.

"They'll never have those records anyway," Bill scoffed.

Helen spoke up again. "You do as Paul says," she told him. "Tell him the name of the hospital you were in."

Bill hesitated, looking at them all in turn. And then sullenly, as if he'd been trapped into it, he said: "San Francisco General."

"Thanks." Paul took it down. "I'll see what I can find out."

"How long do you expect to keep me in here?" Bill wanted to know.

"That depends on how your X-ray plates turn out tomorrow," Paul said, "and on a few other things as well. The main thing is to relax and get a good night's sleep." The young doctor smiled at Helen. "I'll see you later."

He and Rita went out and gave Helen a few minutes alone with her husband. Rita had been lucky enough to locate Paul at his office, and he had come back to the hospital to take care of Bill Ferguson.

They stood by the window at the end of the corridor outside Bill's room, and she looked up at him. "How is he?" she asked.

"I've given him a stiff injection," Paul said. "He'll doze off soon and get a good night's sleep, probably the first one he's had in a long time."

Her eyes had a serious light in them. "He looks wretched," she said. "He must have been suffering terribly."

"And unnecessarily," Paul reminded her. "I begged him to come to my office a month ago."

She sighed and stared out the window at the view of the lawn with its towering elms. "I know all that. Will he be any better to-morrow?"

"The pain will still be there," Paul said. "I'll have to keep him under sedatives most of the time."

Rita glanced up into the young doctor's

stern face again. "Do you suppose he gave you the right name of the hospital?"

He shrugged. "It could very well have been the San Francisco General. We'll soon know. I'm going to put a long distance call through to them when I go back to my office and ask them to send me that material by air mail."

"What if they've never heard of a Bill Ferguson?"

"I'll ask him to tell me the truth," Paul said. "He's run as far as he's going to. This is the end of the line."

"There was that other name," Rita said, trying to recall it, "the one Helen found on the driver's license. I remember now — Wallace Fuller. If the hospital hasn't any records under Bill's own name, hadn't you better check that one?"

Paul wrote down the name on the same slip on which he'd scribbled the name of the hospital. He sighed as he put the paper back in his upper jacket pocket. "I suppose I'll have to. And it's hard to say what might come out of that."

"What else can we do?" Rita worried.

"Not a thing," the young doctor said. And with a glance toward the room, he added: "You'd better drive her home with you. He'll be going to sleep shortly. There's nothing she can do here."

Rita had endured many a difficult situation but none more trying than the drive from the hospital to the Ferguson cottage. Helen had made up her mind to leave the youngsters with her mother for the night, and now she had fallen into a dull, depressed mood. She stared vacantly out the side window of the car as they drove along and said very little.

"Paul is going to try to get in touch with San Francisco tonight," she said. "If he can contact the right party, he might have the plates and case history on Bill here within a day."

Helen sighed. "Don't count on it," she said. "I doubt if Bill ever was in that hospital. And if he was it probably was under another name."

"You seem very sure of that," Rita said, her eyes on the traffic and road ahead.

"After the way he's acted, how can I help but be?" Helen said despondently. "I know he's been trying to hide something, and I'm afraid to think what it could be."

"I'm sure you're making too much of this," Rita said.

"I know something is wrong," her friend said. "I don't know what. Whatever it is, I'll stand by him. I'm just afraid for the children."

"Paul will call me as soon as he finds out anything," Rita said. "And I'll let you know right away. In the meantime, don't imagine a lot of crazy things that probably aren't true!"

Helen refused an invitation to go to Rita's cottage for dinner. One of the men from the office had driven Bill's station wagon home, and it was on the driveway.

"I'd rather get a bite on my own," the stout woman told Rita as she got out of the car. "Then I'll drive to Mother's and help her with the children. They'll go to bed more readily if I'm there. And afterward we can talk."

"If I hear anything meanwhile, I'll call your mother's," Rita promised.

"Do that." Helen tried to smile. "I don't know how to thank you and Paul for all that you've done."

"Don't think about it," Rita said.

She had a leisurely meal, and when she looked outside again it had started to rain. She decided to fill in the time by washing her hair. It would be no problem to dry it before Paul arrived. He'd undoubtedly be at the office until after nine. A wry smile crossed her face as she wondered if Dr. Mary Grant might decide she needed Paul for some sort of conference. In that case, she might as well go to bed and forget he'd promised to come.

But he arrived a little before ten. She had finished drying her hair and was working in the kitchen when he came in. He slipped off his raincoat and brushed back his wet hair.

"Nasty night," he said. "It's starting to come down in sheets."

Rita looked at him and knew he'd heard something by the expression on his face. She tried to keep herself from becoming excited. "What about the calls?" she asked.

He stood with his hands in his trousers pockets and eyed her. "You were right," he said. "Nothing about Ferguson. I had to make two calls."

"And?"

"And they did have the records on Wallace Fuller," Paul said. "I asked them to send them on. There's no doubt Bill and Wallace Fuller are one and the same man."

"But why?" Rita asked.

"I don't know," Paul sighed. "But I'll bet you one thing. We'll be having a call from the police real soon."

"What makes you so sure?"

"The way the fellow at the hospital spoke when he found the records," Paul said. "I have a suspicion there was some sort of card attached to them, asking the hospital to contact the police with any information concerning queries."

"In that case the police will be coming to see you," Rita said. She shook her head. "Well, at least we know now he did change his name."

"And we should soon know why," Paul said. "I'm almost afraid to find out. I like Bill, and Helen's a nice girl, not to mention those wonderful kids. Why would he do a thing like this to her — marry her and burden her and their youngsters with a past he's ashamed of?"

Rita shrugged. "I suppose he loved her and hoped this would never come out."

"He tried hard enough to keep it a secret," Paul said grimly. "He must have suffered every kind of torture with that back. And we still don't know what's ahead for him, what the trouble is."

"What rotten luck some people have!" she said, and thought that despondency was catching. She now felt as depressed as Helen had earlier.

"We'll get the plates tomorrow night or the next morning," Paul said. "And by that time we'll have made our tests at the hospital. If it means an operation, I don't want to delay it an extra day."

She gave him an alarmed glance. "You

haven't seen anything to indicate it might be a malignancy?" she said.

"I don't know," he told her. "I don't know. But I never want a delay when there's a doubt."

Now a new thought struck her, and she asked: "What will we tell Helen? I said I'd call her at her mother's."

Bill stared at her for a moment. "Tell her I got the information. I wouldn't say anything yet about it being under a different name. If the police come into this, she'll know soon enough, and if they don't, we'll just consider it a lucky break."

Rita saw the logic of his argument. "All right," she said, and started for the phone. Then she turned and looked at him with a strange expression on her pretty features. "Isn't it dreadful?" she said. "No matter how this turns out, we can never feel the same about Bill again."

"I suppose not," he said.

"If the police don't follow it up, we'll never be certain why he changed his name," she went on. "And we'll wonder just how much of a criminal he was."

The following day was the beginning of a long period of tension for Rita, although it began quietly enough. It was another of the brilliant days of sunshine that had marked most of the summer. With Laura Graham away, she found herself extremely busy in spurts, but the hospital not being filled to capacity, she had some moments of respite.

It was during one of these that old Dr. Solomon came in with his usual slow, cautious gait. He nodded and said: "I'm canceling an appendectomy that was to come in tomorrow, and I'm also not going to do Mrs. Purdy, the stripping and ligation for varicose veins. Will you please take her off the list?"

Rita nodded and studied him with puzzled eyes. "Are you taking a few days' vacation, Doctor?"

"No." His answer was short and indicated he wanted to discuss the matter no further. He turned to leave and then at the door paused to tell her: "The appendectomy patient's name is Bruce Welsford." And with a slight bow of the iron-gray head, he vanished.

Rita went down her list and drew a line through the names of the patients. Before going to the cafeteria for lunch, she went upstairs to visit Bill Ferguson a moment. She found the stricken Bill restless and seemingly in a good deal of pain. The room was bright with sunlight, and she noted that the glare was falling full across the bed and must be bothering him. She went across and pulled the shade down enough to protect him.

"Your own nurse should have looked after that," she said, coming back to his bedside with a smile. "I think we were better trained. Each year the students here seem to care a little less."

Bill managed a rueful grin. "I've got a sweet little gal taking care of me," he said. "So suppose she does let me get sunburned a bit? You're getting old and cranky."

"How is it with you?" she asked.

He shook his head on the pillow. "They gave me a rough morning. X-rays and tests. Really got the back going."

"You've seen Paul, then?" she said.

"Yes. He spent a lot of time on the tests," Bill told her.

She smiled. "Probably the worst is over. And Helen will be sure to get in this afternoon."

Bill nodded and closed his eyes briefly as if in pain. Then he said: "What about the records from San Francisco? Has Paul done anything about them?"

Rita was instantly on her guard. She said: "Did he say anything to you about them?"

"No." Bill now stared up at her with worried eyes. "But I thought you'd probably know."

"I imagine he's sent an air mail letter or wire," she hedged. "It could take some time, you know. Your accident happened a long time ago."

The man in the bed looked less worried. "You're right," he said. "I doubt if they'll be able to find any records at all."

She managed a smile. "In that case, Paul will go ahead on his own."

Bill gave a small moan as he turned. "That's what he should have done in the first place."

Rita left him, promising to come back again before she went home. She took the elevator to the cafeteria, her mind filled with the conversation she'd just had with Bill.

She entered the cafeteria, looking for Paul, and stood in the doorway for a moment as she glanced around the crowded room. Then she saw him! He and Dr. Mary Grant were seated at a table for two, and their heads were bent together in a manner that suggested an extremely intimate conversation. For a moment she felt humiliation and a touch of anger. She'd been wanting to talk to Paul so badly, and here he was with another woman!

Then she realized her attitude was immature and emotional. What she was actually looking at was a serious discussion between the two senior members of the hospital staff. Had she any right to interpret it otherwise? With some misgivings still remaining, she took a tray and went about selecting her lunch.

Paul had not turned up at her office by the time she left to pick up the floor sheets. And she again stopped in Bill's room before coming downstairs in the hope of finding him there. But instead she met Helen and the children, who were strangely quiet at seeing their father in bed in the middle of the day and in a strange place. Rita had little chance to talk with Helen, but she saw Bill had been given some sedation and was in a languid, more restful mood. It was the best thing for him at this time.

The day ended and she went home, feeling depressed and strangely alone.

And she was even more depressed when, instead of coming over that night, Paul called her on the phone. He seemed different and in an abstracted mood, as if the very call itself had been difficult for him.

"I can't make it to your place after office hours," he told her. "I have to go back to the hospital."

She couldn't hide the bitterness in her voice. "That sounds familiar."

"Rita, I have to do it," he insisted wearily.

"I've been wanting to talk to you all day," she said.

"Is there anything I should know?"

"No," she said fully. "I guess it really isn't important."

"I'll come by the office tomorrow sure," he promised.

"Give Mary Grant my regards," she said.

Paul sounded annoyed. "There's no need of that!"

She sighed. "You must be busy. I won't keep you." And she hung up.

It was already dark outside. She went into the living room and, feeling completely miserable, sank down on the end of the divan as large tears formed at the corners of her eyes and streamed down her cheeks. Then, holding her face in her hands, she began to weep aloud.

She was feeling so unhappy and withdrawn the next morning she hardly answered Winnie's nod as she passed by the telephone operator's post. As she made her way back from the dressing room to her own office, she saw Dr. Jonas Arbo and Dr. Solomon in serious discussion in the lobby, but it made no impression on her. She was too deep in her own misery.

But when she went into her office and discovered Laura Graham had returned and was seated at her desk, she knew something unusual was in the air. Laura had still a week's holidays left.

Coming out of her fog of gloom, she asked: "What are you doing back?"

The white-haired woman gave her a curious glance. "Don't tell me you haven't heard? Emergency! They've called everybody in."

Rita stared at her as she sat down. "What sort of emergency?"

Laura Graham looked grim. "The very worst from a hospital viewpoint. A whole section of the third floor is crawling with staph infection. It started among the post-operative patients, and now nearly every patient has been hit."

"Oh, no!" Rita exclaimed.

"It's a lot easier to get than get rid of," Laura Graham went on. "All that area has been blocked off. Nurses and doctors working there will have to use a special sterile technique. Masks will have to be worn while they are in there and everything changed when they leave. No visitors for the desperately ill and a general line of complaints all day long. We're in for a time!"

Rita found it hard to believe. "Isn't that going to mean a lot of time lost and extra help needed?"

Laura Graham opened her eyes wide. "Why else do you suppose I'm here? And I understand Dr. Grant is going to put some of Ellen May Barry's new Hospital Aid group into service on the second floor. That's clean so far, and it will relieve extra nurses for upstairs."

"How do they go about fighting a thing like this?"

"It could take some time," Laura Graham said. "One thing is certain. They'll keep operations to a minimum. And you'd understand why if you had seen the number of staph infection ulcerations I've come across in my day. More patients die of the infection than the surgery."

"And not even antibiotics help?"

The older woman shrugged. "Those germs send 'fifth columnists' everywhere. They're here in the air we breathe, the dust that settles on the food we eat, the furniture we sit on, the beds we sleep in. They're everywhere! The only answer is to keep the present cases contained and to guard against further infection. In brief, what I said in the beginning — sterile technique!" Her phone rang, and she turned to answer it.

Rita found herself engaged in a new type of routine. Mimeographed bulletins were handed out to various departments with a list of detailed instructions to follow in the emergency. Again she felt ashamed, knowing that Dr. Mary Grant and Paul had undoubtedly worked on these all last night. If only he'd given her a hint! But she supposed the doctors didn't want to sound an alarm, even to the staff, until they were certain. News of a widespread hospital infection of this dangerous type always caused a certain amount of panic. It became more pronounced when patients were not allowed visitors. Already bulletins had been sent to newspapers, radio and television stations, announcing the emergency at Riverdale Memorial.

Chapter Twelve

It took a full moment for the impact of the words to sink in. Then she leaned back on the desk and said faintly: "When?"

"It happened last night," Paul said. "There are all sorts of rescue parties out, of course. They've not completely lost hope yet. But the submarine dived very deep, and there's been no word from her since. At that depth, rescue is almost out of the question."

"I can't believe it," she said, shaking her head.

"Everyone is shocked," the young doctor said quietly. "It's the first sub operating out of the Portsmouth Navy Yard to have any trouble."

A new thought crossed Rita's mind. She said: "I must call Jack's mother-in-law. I have her number here somewhere." And she went back to her desk and rummaged through lists until she found it. Then she put the call through as Paul stood by

189

waiting. The phone rang again and again, but there was no answer.

At last she put the receiver down. "I seem to remember Jack telling me something about her going to visit a brother in Boston," she said. And then, with a pleading glance at Paul: "I still can't believe it!"

He raised a placating hand. "There's nothing to be gained by dwelling on it," he said. "Good word may come through any time."

"Should I call the naval base?" she wondered.

"I don't know what good it would do," he said. "But suit yourself. Do you want any lunch?"

She shook her head. "I would like some coffee, if you'd bring it up with you."

"I'll be back shortly," he promised, and left.

Laura Graham returned from her lunch. The white-haired woman glanced at Rita and knew at once she'd heard the news. "You know about the *Alcestis*," she said.

Rita nodded. "Isn't it dreadful!"

The older woman sat at her desk wearily. "It seems be the week for disasters. I heard the latest bulletin on the radio before I came in. Another coast guard cutter with special electronic equipment for getting signals from deep water has joined the search."

"Then there may still be a chance," Rita said, clinging desperately to any hope. It was too cruel that the boyish Jack should die this way.

"The best hope is that the *Alcestis* may be able to repair its damage and make the journey to the surface," Laura Graham told her. "According to the news, these new atomic subs operate at such depths it's almost impossible to conduct rescue operations from another vessel."

Their conversation was terminated by Dr. Paul Reid's return with her coffee. He also brought along a cellophane-wrapped package of cookies. "You may feel the need of these later," he warned.

"Thanks." Rita managed a faint smile. "Did you get the information from San Francisco?"

"No. But we won't need it," Paul said. "The new plates we took yesterday showed the trouble plainly enough. There's a growth in the spinal area. Dr. Solomon and I are going to operate tomorrow."

"Won't that be risky, with this infection running wild?" she asked.

Paul shrugged. "It will be riskier not to. I don't like the look of it. We'll have to take the chance."

Laura Graham shook her head. "I'm glad

it's not me you're wheeling in there. I've seen too many festering staph ulcers in incisions."

"I want to get the operation over with before there are any more developments," Paul said. "Morton Gordon, Jr. has called an emergency meeting of the hospital board tomorrow night; he's saying we should close the operating room down."

Laura Graham frowned. "But that's nonsense. We might as well lock all the doors and go home if we aren't going to continue functioning."

"Try and explain that to him," Paul said gloomily.

Laura gave her a knowing glance. "Remember what I told you," she said. "They aren't going to miss this opportunity to cause trouble."

She nodded. "You were right." And to Paul: "Have you let Helen know about Bill's operation?"

"I'm going to phone and tell her now," Paul said, still hesitating by her desk. "You feel all right?"

Rita sighed. "Yes. Let me know if you hear anything more."

He left, promising he would. And now it seemed the lagging tempo of the past few weeks had changed in a frantic way. The hospital switchboard was loaded with calls from worried relatives, wanting to know when they could visit the hospital. Complaints poured in from every source, and Rita found herself operating in a general area of confusion.

Two emergency patients were admitted and given rooms on the second floor where no infection had appeared as yet. But space there was rapidly filling up. Rita was already worrying about what she would do in the days ahead.

And she couldn't get her mind off the submarine disaster and Jack Thomas. She made several visits to Winnie at the switchboard to see if she'd heard any news.

The hatchet-faced woman gave her a despairing wave. "I haven't had a minute to listen to my radio," she said. She always kept a small transistor by her switchboard. "You take it if you want to."

Rita carried the little radio back to her desk and kept it on at a low level. The bulletins on the disaster were frequent and monotonous, without any good news. She left it on for Laura Graham to listen to while she went upstairs to collect the daily reports.

When she re-entered her office, Laura Graham rose excitedly. "Long distance has been trying to get you," she said. "I tried to locate you on the third, but you had left. You're to call back Operator 17."

Rita's first thought was this would be Jack's mother-in-law trying to reach her. She sat back at her desk and had Winnie connect her with long distance. She asked for the proper operator and then waited for the call to be put through, wondering what she could say to console this woman twice bereaved in a few weeks.

But when the voice came through from the other end of the line, she was both shocked and delighted. It was Jack Thomas himself she heard. "I knew you'd be worried," he said, sounding far away. "This is the first chance I've had to put in a call. I happened not to be on the *Alcestis* run yesterday."

Rita's voice rose in her excitement. "I'm so glad, Jack, so thankful! You don't know how I've worried."

"It's an awful thing," he said. "I'm afraid there isn't much hope for the boys aboard."

"I know," she said. "I felt that from the radio bulletins."

"I won't hold the line any longer," Jack said. "I'll be seeing you soon."

She put down the phone with reverent gratitude. She looked over at Laura Graham, who was waiting to hear more.

"He's safe," she said. "He wasn't assigned to the trial run yesterday."

Laura Graham smiled. "You see? I told you not to worry so much. Now you can concentrate on our troubles here."

And as soon as she had phoned Paul and told him the good news, she did. There was plenty to do. The volume of phone inquiries continued all through the day, and she stayed on at the hospital until nearly five o'clock.

She drove home in the warm sun of the September afternoon. It was too late to think of swimming, but a walk along the beach would be refreshing.

She left her car and strolled slowly along the road in the waning sunshine. It was still pleasantly warm, and she took a deep breath of the country air.

There was no one in sight on the beach, and she walked down to the water's edge for several minutes. Then she made her way across the fine white sand.

"Don't be in such a hurry!" a familiar male voice called from behind her.

She stopped and turned to find herself facing Cliff Thomson.

The usual arrogant smile crossed the coarsely handsome face. "This is good luck," he said. "I've missed you lately."

"I'm on my way home now," she said.

He stood directly in her path. "Surely you have a few minutes to talk with a good friend."

Rita looked at him with cool eyes. "I'm not certain you fit that description."

He laughed. "Well, it will do." And then: "How are things shaping up at the hospital?"

"We're managing," she said.

"Not very well, according to what I heard," Cliff told her in his familiar know-it-all fashion. "Morton Gordon, Jr. says the place is alive with the plague. I guess that Dr. Mary Grant has gotten herself and the hospital in a real fix!"

"She's done very well," Rita protested.

"Loyalty is all right," the big man told her. "But that's carrying it too far." There was a knowing light in his pale blue eyes. "I'll bet you've seen a lot of things the board would like to know. Why not pass some of them on? I'd see they got to the right ears."

Rita smiled at him derisively. "I'll bet you would! No, thanks! I'm not that interested in your political ambitions."

She saw his face crimson. His broad face was less jovial now. "You're backing the wrong horse," he said. "I hope you know that."

She shook her head. "No. I did that just

once. Since then I've learned my lesson." And she made her way around him. She walked on without looking back until she reached her car.

When she entered the driveway, Helen's station wagon was already there, and she saw her friend sitting in the verandah settee. She got out of her car and quickly mounted the steps.

"I didn't see you when I first came up," she said. "Have you been waiting here long?"

Helen shook her head. The stout girl's face plainly showed the strain of the past few days. There were worry wrinkles at her forehead and around her eyes and mouth.

She said: "My mother is at our place looking after the children. I wanted to ask you about Bill. I wasn't allowed to see him today."

"It's the infection," Rita said with a frown. "You know about it."

Helen nodded. "Yes. They say it's terrible, that a lot of people may die from it. And Morton Gordon, Jr. is holding a special meeting tomorrow night to try to stop them doing any more operations."

"A lot of that is just hysteria," Rita explained. "But it is bad enough. Paul knows the risks and he thinks it's wise to operate on

Bill in the morning. Dr. Solomon is going to assist."

"But if there's real danger —" Helen protested weakly.

"There is danger in waiting as well," Rita told her.

"I suppose I should agree with what Paul thinks best," Helen faltered. "But I've worried so I hardly know which way to turn." She paused. "Has he had any word from San Francisco?"

"Not yet," Rita said. "But he no longer needs that material."

"Perhaps it is better this way," Helen said with a sigh of resignation. And then, facing Rita with pleading eyes, she said: "You don't really think Bill did something awful out there, that he is a criminal?"

"I can't imagine him being involved in anything wrong," Rita said truthfully. "I've told you that before."

Helen rose to go. "I know," she said quietly. "But I can't get it out of my mind. I hope some day he tells me."

"I'm sure he will," Rita said, walking out to the station wagon with her. "Just now the main thing is to see him through tomorrow."

She had parked her car to one side so Helen could get out easily. Now she watched the stout girl back into the main road and waved her on her way. Then she went back into the house and prepared dinner for herself before settling down with a book.

She'd been reading for more than an hour when she heard a car come in the driveway. She got up with pleasurable anticipation and went over and turned on the outside porch light. But when she opened the screen door, it was not Paul who stood on the verandah, but Dr. Mary Grant.

She smiled at Rita. "I hope I haven't disturbed you. I thought I'd come by for a late coffee."

Rita returned the smile and stood back for her to enter. "I'm glad you came. I've been here by myself all evening."

Dr. Mary Grant looked chic as usual in a dark two-piece suit.

When they were seated with coffee, the young woman doctor said: "I heard that your friend wasn't on board the *Alcestis*. I know you must be very thankful."

Rita nodded. "I couldn't believe it when I first heard his voice."

"Have you known him long?"

"No," Rita said. "Not really. But we became very good friends through his wife, who was a patient at the hospital. A sweet girl."

"So I've heard." Mary Grant looked down at her cup.

Rita was surprised by her unexpected visit but didn't want to show it.

She said: "I've tried to help him. He's very boyish and nice. He doesn't seem to have too many friends."

"I understand," the young woman doctor said, lifting her eyes to meet Rita's. "You two are friends in the same way as Paul and myself."

Rita laughed lightly. "I suppose that is a good way to describe it."

"Paul has worked very hard to help me since I came here," Mary Grant went on. "We've spent so much time together I've begun to worry you might misinterpret it."

"Not really," Rita said.

Dr. Mary Grant smiled ruefully. "It wouldn't be strange if you should. And that's why I'm here: to tell you you have no need to worry."

"I know," Rita said. "At least I've known since this morning. I should have realized earlier." She paused and looked down at her hands. "I had a rather bad experience when I first came to Riverdale. Perhaps it left me open to suspicions." She looked up at the woman doctor with a smile. "I'm over them now."

"You've found Riverdale a difficult place to live, then?"

"I like Riverdale," Rita said with a smile. "But like any other small city its size, it has many faults."

Dr. Mary Grant's intelligent eyes took on a thoughtful expression. "I hoped when I came here I'd be able to accomplish my best work. Now it seems I'm not wanted and won't be allowed to stay."

"A lot of people are glad you came," Rita protested.

Mary Grant smiled. "Certainly not Morton Gordon, Jr. If I had known his attitude and the position in which my coming has put Glen as mayor, I wouldn't have thought of applying for the job."

"They can't blame you for this staph infection thing," Rita said. "And aside from that, everything you've done has been for the betterment of the hospital."

The woman doctor put her cup on the table and stood up. "I'm afraid I'll be blamed for many things tomorrow night," she said. "But at least I wanted to be sure that everything was right between you and Paul, and between you and me as well."

It was a generous gesture on Dr. Mary Grant's part and bestowed at a moment of crisis when her mind was probably much

more on other things. But it was character-
istic of the talented young woman that she
should think of Rita.

The following morning's weather suggested the pattern of the day to follow. It was
gray, with a threat of storm. Rita shivered
slightly as she walked from her car to the entrance of the hospital. The ominous cloudy
skies were not a pleasant omen. She thought
that within a matter of minutes Paul and Dr.
Solomon would be standing by the operating table, ready to begin with Bill. She
considered the many hazards involved and
was worried.

The entire hospital seemed touched with
an atmosphere of gloom. All the staff had
seen the notice of the board meeting, and all
had been affected by the new regulations in
the fight against the staph infection that
stubbornly seemed to be hanging on. The
only good news came from the second floor,
where no new cases had yet been reported.

Laura Graham greeted Rita with a wan
smile. "Your friend, Mrs. Ferguson, is here,"
she said. "She'll be staying until after her
husband's operation. She's in the large waiting room off the lobby."

"I'll look in on her," Rita promised.

Helen sat huddled in an easy chair, the
picture of despair. When Rita came in, she

glanced up at her, a trace of fear spreading across her face. "Any news?"

Rita gave her a smile of reassurance. "It will be some time yet," she said. "And the doctors will no longer be coming down, as they're taking special precautions."

As it turned out, it was almost noon before Rita saw Paul. He came into the office with the kind of assurance in his manner that told her he was satisfied with the way it had gone.

"I've talked with Helen," he said. "Dr. Solomon is still with her. It went all right. We got it all, and I'm strongly inclined to believe it wasn't a malignancy. Of course we can't be sure until the lab report comes in."

She sat back with a smile. "Another crisis over with."

"Provided he doesn't pick up staph or some other bug," Paul said. And then, with a wise look in his eyes: "I hear you had a visitor last night."

"It certainly wasn't you," Rita teased him.

"I was here making my midnight rounds." He smiled. "I think it is about time you two got together, anyhow." And he started for the door.

"Paul!" she called after him.

He turned. "Yes?"

"How will it go tonight?"

His rugged young face was serious. "It doesn't look good. But we'll put up a stiff fight."

Bill Ferguson was put in one of the several rooms on the second floor that had been reserved for surgical patients during the emergency period. Rita called the floor nurse, and the report was good. He was coming out of the effects of the anesthesia with no complications and seemed to be resting as well as could be expected.

All day there were a steady stream of visitors to the administrative office. Once Rita saw Mayor Glen Parent come by the door. He waved to her, and smiled. Later Morton Gordon, Jr. strode importantly into the lobby, accompanied by none other than Cliff Thomson. Cliff looked surprisingly young and awkward at the pompous older man's side. He didn't see Rita, and she was glad.

Later, Laura Graham told her: "Our side has had a minor victory. They've swung Dr. Solomon to their point of view."

"And Morton Gordon, Jr. has been counting on him," Rita said.

The older nurse nodded. "I know. But he couldn't stomach the unfairness of blaming Dr. Grant for this infection."

Rita sighed. "It's too bad it couldn't have

been cleared up before tonight's meeting."

"Now you're asking the impossible." Laura Graham chuckled. "Be satisfied with lesser miracles. It may be all we need."

Rita met Paul in the lobby on her way home. The young doctor was heading in the direction of the administrative offices. He said: "Want to endure another long evening of waiting?"

She smiled. "I'm used to them."

"Fine," he nodded. "I'll be over sure after the meeting. But it mightn't be until twelve or later."

Actually, it was later. When a tired-looking Paul stepped into the hall to greet her, the clock showed twelve-thirty. Rita faced him for a moment without saying anything, trying to read his face.

He broke into a smile and took her by the arms. "Ellen May Barry and her husband were at the meeting," he said. "And she told me to tell you we'd won the snowball fight."

"Oh, Paul!" she exclaimed, falling happily against him.

Later, as they sat on the divan together, he told her the details. "It was Dr. Solomon who deserves the credit," he exulted. "I never realized that little old gentleman was such a ferocious fighter. He made Morton

Gordon, Jr.'s arguments look like kid stuff!"

"Wonderful," Rita said with a smile.

"And by the way," Paul said, with a teasing glance, "your dear friend Cliff Thomson got up to speak for his side, and I think his political future died right there on the platform. He's even slower-minded than Morton Gordon, Jr."

"So Dr. Mary Grant continues as superintendent!"

"Better than that, I don't think she'll have any more opposition." He paused. "I checked on Bill before I left. He's doing fine."

Rita had been leaning close to him. Now she sat up. "I must call Helen. I told her I would if you came."

Paul gave her a strange look. "By the way, the police came today. They arrived at the same time as the X-ray plates from San Francisco. I was able to put them off until Bill is better."

She felt a surge of sorrow. "Poor Bill! What is the story behind it all?"

"Not as bad as it could be," Paul said. "He had an alcoholic wife. A year before his accident, he walked out on her. After the accident, he came here and changed his name and married Helen." He paused to note Rita's worried expression. "Yes. That made him a bigamist, and that was what he was afraid of us finding out. But what he didn't know was that his first wife died approximately three months before his second marriage. So with the exception of making his present name legal and explaining to the police, I'd say he is in the clear."

Rita's face became radiantly happy. "The last problem settled," she said.

He smiled and drew her to him. "Except a marriage in October." And he kissed her.

We hope you have enjoyed this Large Print book. Other Thorndike, Wheeler or Chivers Press Large Print books are available at your library or directly from the publishers.

For more information about current and upcoming titles, please call or write, without obligation, to:

Publisher
Thorndike Press
295 Kennedy Memorial Drive
Waterville, ME 04901
Tel. (800) 223-1244

Or visit our Web site at:
www.gale.com/thorndike
www.gale.com/wheeler

OR

Chivers Large Print
published by BBC Audiobooks Ltd
St James House, The Square
Lower Bristol Road
Bath BA2 3SB
England
Tel. +44(0) 800 136919
email: bbcaudiobooks@bbc.co.uk
www.bbcaudiobooks.co.uk

All our Large Print titles are designed for easy reading, and all our books are made to last.